'Stop in the ♥ name of pants!'

Fab New Confessions of

Georgia Nicolson

The Confessions of Georgia Nicolson:

Angus, thongs and full-frontal snogging

'It's OK, I'm wearing really big knickers!'

'Knocked out by my nunga-nungas.'

'Dancing in my nuddy-pants!'

'...and that's when it fell off in my hand.'

'...then he ate my boy entrancers.'

'...startled by his furry shorts!'

'Luuurve is a many trousered thing...'

'Stop in the name of pants!'

Also available on tape and CD:

'...and that's when it fell off in my hand.'

'...then he ate my boy entrancers.'

'...startled by his furry shorts!'

'Luuurve is a many trousered thing...'

'Stop in the name of pants!'

'Stop in the ♡name of pants!'

Fab ⭐New Confessions of Georgia Nicolson

Louise Rennison ♥

HarperCollins *Children's Books*

Find out more about Georgia at www.georgianicolson.com

First published in Great Britain in hardback by HarperCollins *Children's Books* 2008
HarperCollins *Children's Books* is a division of HarperCollins*Publishers* Ltd,
77-85 Fulham Palace Road, Hammersmith, London W6 8JB

4

Copyright © Louise Rennison 2008

The author asserts the moral right to be identified as the author of this work.

ISBN-13 978-0-00-727583-0
ISBN-10 0-00-727583-8

Printed and bound in England by
Clays Ltd, St Ives plc

Mixed Sources
Product group from well-managed
forests and other controlled sources
www.fsc.org Cert no. SW-COC-1806
© 1996 Forest Stewardship Council
FSC

FSC is a non-profit international organisation established to promote the
responsible management of the world's forests. Products carrying the FSC
label are independently certified to assure consumers that they come
from forests that are managed to meet the social, economic and
ecological needs of present and future generations.

Find out more about HarperCollins and the environment at
www.harpercollins.co.uk/green

To my groovy and fabby and marvy family and mates (including my extended family at HarperCollins and Aitken Alexander).

'Stop in the name of pants!' – my latest work of geniosity – is dedicated especially to absent mates. Who have selfishly gone off to have fun. (Yes, you know who you are, Jeddbox and Elton.)

And also to absent mates who aren't really absent but lurking about somewhere pretending to be absent.

A Note from Georgia

Dear chums, chumettes and, er... chummly wummlies,

I write to you from my bed of pain. Once again I have exhausted myself with creativitosity writing 'Stop in the Name of Pants!' I am having to lie down with a cup of tea and a Curly Wurly. But that is how vair vair much I care about you all, my little pallies. I am a fool to myself, I know.

I ask only one thing in return and that is this. All of you must dance the Viking disco hornpipe extravaganza in classrooms and recreation facilities throughout the world. It doesn't matter if there are only two or three of you, just stand up proudly, get your horns and paddles out (oo-er) and dance!!!

Loads and loads of deep luuurve,

Georgia
XXX

p.s. Some of you don't know what the Viking disco hornpipe extravaganza is, do you?

p.p.s. Please don't tell me you didn't know that Vikings had discos.

p.p.p.s. Or that they shouted "Hooooorrrn!!!"

p.p.p.p.s. For those of you who haven't bothered to keep up with my diaries because you are just TOO BUSY, I have put instructions for the dance at the back near the glossary.

p.p.p.p.p.s. What have you been TOO BUSY doing?

p.p.p.p.p.p.s. I suppose you have been TOO BUSY to even know what the having-the-hump scale is as well.

p(x7).s. So I have included that at the back too. My so-called friend Jas (who has the hump pretty much all of the time) would be at number four with you by now (cold-shoulderosity work).

p(x8).s. I really luuurve you and do not mind that you are lazy minxes. That is your special charm. Pip pip. X

Deep in the forest of red-bottomosity

Saturday July 30th
Camping fiasco
11:30 p.m.

In my tent of shame.

Again.

The rest of my so-called pals are still out in the woods with the lads and I have crept back to the campsite aloney. I can hear snoring from Miss Wilson's tent and also Herr Kamyer's. I bet there will be a deputation of voles coming along shortly to complain that they can't get any sleep because of the racket.

11:32 p.m.

I'm going to forget about everything and just go to sleep in my lovely sleeping bag. On the lovely soft ground. Not. It's like sleeping on an ironing board. And I do know what that is like actually.

11:33 p.m.

I said coming on this school camping trip would be a fiasco of a sham and I was not wrong.

11:34 p.m.
I was right.

11:35 p.m.
I wonder what the others are doing?

11:36 p.m.
Anyway, the main thing is that I am now, officially, the girlfriend of a Luuurve God. And therefore I have put my red bottom behind me with a firm hand. I will never again be found wandering lonely as a clud into the cakeshop of luuurve. Or picking up some other éclair or tart or fondant

fancy. Ditto Eccles cakes and Spotty dick or... shut up, brain.

11:37 p.m.

So, speaking as the official girlfriend of a Luuurve God who has put my red bottom behind me with a firm hand and who will never be wandering around looking for extra cakes, can someone tell me this...

How in the name of God's pantyhose have I ended up snogging Dave the Laugh?

Also known as Dave the Tart.

Two minutes later

Oh goddy god god. And let us face facts. It wasn't just a matey type snog. You know, not a – "It's all right, mate, I'm just a mate accidentally snogging another mate" – sort of snog.

It was, frankly and to get to the point and not beat around the whatsit, a "phwoooaar" snogging situation.

Thirty seconds later

In fact, it was deffo number four and about to be number five.

Four seconds later

Anyway, shut up, brain, I must think. Now is not the time for a rambling trip to Ramble Land. Now is the time to put my foot down with a firm hand and stop snogging my not-boyfriend Dave the Laugh.

One minute later

I mean, I am practically married to Masimo the Luuurve God.

Ten seconds later

Well, give or take him actually asking me to marry him.

Five seconds later

And the fact that he has gone off to Pizza-a-gogo land on holiday and left me here in Merrie but dangerous England to fend for myself. Being made to go on stupid school camping trips with madmen (Miss Wilson and Herr Kamyer).

He has left me here, wandering around defenceless in the wilderness near Ramsgate, miles away from the nearest TopShop.

Three seconds later

And how can I help it if Dave the Laugh burrows into my tent?

Because that is more or less what happened. That is *le* fact.

I was snuggling down under some bit of old raincoat (or sleeping bag, as Jas would say in her annoying *oooh isn't it fun outdoors* sort of way). Anyway, where was I? Oh yes, I was snuggling down earlier tonight after an action-packed day of newt drawing when there was a *tap-tap-tapping* on the side of the tent. I thought it might have been an owl attack but it was Dave the Laugh and his Barmy Army (Tom, Declan, Sven and Edward) enticing us into their tent with promises of snacks and light entertainment.

Four seconds later

I blame Dave entirely for this. He and I are just mates and I have a boyfriend and he has a girlfriend and that is that, end of story. Not. Because then he comes to the countryside looking for me and waving his Horn about.

We were frolicking around in the lads' tent, and Dave and me went off for an innocent walk in the woods. You know, like old matey-type mates do. But then I put my foot down a bloody badger hole or something and fell backwards into the river. Anyway, Dave was laughing like a loon for a bit before he reached down and put his arms around me to lift me up the riverbank and I said, "I think I may have broken my bottom."

And he was really smiling and then he said, "Oh bugger it, it has to be done."

And he snogged me.

When he stopped I pushed him backwards and looked at him. I was giving him my worst look.

He said, "What?"

I said, "You know what. Don't just say 'what' like that."

"Like what?"

I said, with enormous dignitosity, "Look, you enticed me with your shenanigans and, erm, puckering stuff."

He said, "Erm, I think you will find that you agreed to come to my tent in the middle of the night to steal me from my girlfriend."

I said, "It was you that snogged me."

He looked at me and then he sighed. "Yeah, I know. I don't feel very good about this. I'm not so... well, you're used to it."

My head nearly exploded. "I'm USED to what??"

He looked quite angry, which felt horrible. I'd seen him angry with me before and I didn't usually like what he had to say. He went on: "You started all this sounding the Horn business ages ago, using me like a decoy duck and then going out with Robbie, then messing about with me and then going out with Masimo. And then telling me that you felt mixed up."

I just looked at him. I felt a bit weepy actually. I might as well be wet at both ends.

My eyes filled with tears and I blinked them away and he just kept on looking at me. I couldn't tell what he was thinking. Maybe he had had enough of me and he really hated me.

Then he just walked away and I was left alone. Alone to face the dark woods of my shamenosity and the tutting of Baby Jesus.

Ten seconds later

And I didn't even know which way the tent was.

The trees looked scary and there was all sorts of snuffling going on. Maybe it was rogue pigs. Pigs who had had enough of the farm life, fed up with just bits of old potato peelings to eat and nowhere to poo in privacy. Maybe these ones wanted a change of menu and had made a bid for freedom by scaling the pigpen fence late at night. Or perhaps they were like the prisoners of war in that old film that Vati's always rambling on about. *The Great Escape.* When the prisoners dug a tunnel under the prison fence.

That's what these pigs must have done. Tunnelled out of the farm to freedom.

There was more snuffling.

Yes, but now they were hungry. Runaways from the farm just waiting to pounce on some food. If they found me, they would think of me like I thought of them. As some chops. Some chops in a skirt. In sopping knickers in my case. Out here in the Wild Woods the trotter was on the other foot.

I could climb up a tree.

Could they climb trees?

Could I climb trees?

Oh God, not death by pig!!!

The scuffling got nearer and then a little black thing scampered out of the undergrowth. It was a vole. How much noise can one stupid little mousey thing make? A LOT is the answer.

I should make friends with it really, because with my luck I will be kidnapped by voles and raised as one of their own. On the plus side, I would never have to face the shame of my red-bottomosity, just spend my years digging and licking my fur and being all aloney on my owney.

Like I am now.

Dave appeared out of the darkness in front of me. I ran over to him and burst into tears. He put his arm around me.

"OK, Kittykat, I'm sorry. Come on, it's all right. Stop blubbing. Your nose will get all swollen up and you'll collapse under the weight of your nungas and I can't carry all of you home."

It was nice in the forest now. I could see the moon through the trees. And my hiccups had almost gone. As we walked along he smiled at me and stroked my hair. Oooh, he was nice.

He said, "We haven't done this luuurve business before, so we are bound to be crap at it. I do feel bad about Emma, but that is not your fault. That is my fault. We can put away our Horns and be matey-type mates again. Come on. Cheer up. Be nasty to me again, it's more normal. I like you and I always have and I always will."

I sniffed a bit and gave him a brave, quivering but attractive smile. I kept my nostrils fully under control so that they didn't spread all over my face. As we walked along I could hear little squelching noises coming from the knicker department. With a bit of luck you couldn't hear it above the noise of rustling voles (also known as my nearly adopted family).

Dave said, "Is that your pants squelching, Gee? You should change them when we get back. You don't want to get pneumonia of the bum-oley on top of everything else."

We walked back through the trees in the light of the jolly old big shiny yellow thing, and no, I do not mean an illuminated banana had just appeared, although that would have been good.

Then everything went horrible again; there were some hideous noises coming from the left of us...

"Tom, Tom. over here. I think I've found an owl dropping."

Oh brilliant – Jas, Wild Woman of the Forest, was in the vicinity. Dave took his arm away from my shoulder. I looked up at him, he looked down at me and bent over and kissed me on the mouth really gently.

"Ah well, the end of the line, Kittykat. You go off with your Italian lesbian boyfriend and see how it goes and I'll try and be a good mate to you. Don't tell me too much about you and him because I won't like it – but other than that, let's keep the accidental outburst of red-bottomosity to ourselves."

I smiled at him. "Dave, I..."

"Yes?"

"I think I can feel something moving in my undercrackers."

Midnight

And that is when I scampered off back to Loony Headquarters. That is, our school campsite. To change my nick-nacks.

Ten past midnight

I said to Baby Jesus, "I know I have done wrong and I am sorry times a million, but at least you have been kind enough not to send a plague of tadpoles into my pantaloonies."

Sunday July 31st

11:00 a.m.

I must say, it was a lot easier getting our tent down than up. I pulled all the peg-type things out of the ground, Rosie and Jools kicked the pole over, and though it wouldn't go in its stupid bag thing, we made a nice bundle of it in about three minutes flat.

Jas and her woodland mates and Herr Kamyer and Miss

Wilson were folding and sorting and putting things in little pockets and so on for about a million years.

Ten minutes later

Rosie, Jools and me stashed our tent bundle in the suitcase holder thing at the side of the coach and got on board past Mr Attwood. The only reason we got on without some sort of Nazi investigation and body search was because he was slumped at the wheel with his cap pulled down over his face.

Rosie said, "That's how he drives."

And she is not wrong if the nightmare journey home was anything to go by.

Twenty minutes later

We were having a little zizz on the back seat under a pile of our coats when Jas, patron saint of the Rambling On Society, came on board. I knew that because she came to the back of the coach and shook my shoulder quite violently. I peered at her. She was tremendously red-faced.

I said, "Jas, I am trying to sleep."

"You didn't pack your tent up properly."

I said, "Oh, I'm sorry, are the tent police here?"

She said, "You have just made a big mess of yours in the boot. We had to take it out and pack it up so that we could get ours in!"

"Yes, well, Jas, as you can see, I am very, very busy."

"You are soooo selfish and lax and that is why you have a million boyfriends, none of whom will stay with you."

She stormed off to sit at the front near her besties Miss Wilson and Herr Kamyer.

God, she is annoying, but luckily no one else heard her rambling on about the million boyfriends scenario. I wonder if the boys are home yet?

Five minutes later

Herr Kamyer stood up at the front of the bus and said, "Can I haff your attention, girls." Everyone carried on talking, so he started clapping his hands together.

Mr Attwood jerked to life and said, "It's time to go."

Herr Kamyer said, "*Ja, ja, danke schön, Herr Driver*, but first I vill count zat ve are all pre—"

At which point Mr Attwood put his foot down and Herr Kamyer fell backwards into Miss Wilson's lap.

Quite, quite horrific.

We just watched the young lovers as they got redder and redder. Like red things at a red party.

Herr Kamyer tried to get off her lap, but the coach was being driven so violently by Mr Mad that he kept falling back again, saying, "*Ach*, I am *sehr* sorry I..."

And Miss Wilson was saying, "No, no, it's quite all right. I mean I..."

Eventually, when Mr Attwood was forced to stop at the lights, Herr Kamyer got into his own seat and pretended to be inspecting his moth collection. Miss Wilson got out her knitting but kept looking over at him.

I said to Rosie, "Just remember this – he was there when Nauseating P. Green did her famous falling into the shower tent fiasco and Miss Wilson was exposed to the world having a shower. He has seen Miss Wilson in the nuddy-pants."

I was just thinking about popping back to Snoozeland when Ellen dithered into life.

"Er, Georgia... you know when Jas said... well, when she said that you had... like a million boyfriends or something, I mean have you or something?"

Rosie said, "Ellen, gadzooks and lackaday, OF COURSE Georgia hasn't got a million boyfriends. She would be covered in them if she had."

Ellen said, "Well, I know but, well, I mean, she's only got Masimo, and that is like... well..."

Mabs said, "Yeah, Masimo... and the rest."

I said to Mabs, "Who rattled your cage?"

And Mabs said, "I'm just remarking on the Dave the Laugh factor."

Ellen sat up then. "What Dave the Laugh factor?"

Oh Blimey O'Reilly's nose massager! Here we go again, once more into the bakery of love. I am going to have to nip this Dave the Laugh thing in the bud.

I said, "Ellen, did you snog Declan and, if so, what number did you get up to?"

Ellen looked like she had swallowed a sock full of vole poo, which is not a good look.

"Well, I... well, you know, I, well, do you think I did or something?"

I said, "A yes or no any time this side of the grave would be fab, Ellen."

Ellen said she had to get her cardi from Jas's rucky and

tottered off to sit next to her. Hahahahaha. I am without doubtosity top girlie at red-herringnosity.

4:00 p.m.

Dropped off at the bottom of my road. By some miracle we have arrived home not maimed and crippled by our coach "driver" and school caretaker Elvis Attwood. He hates girls.

I don't think he has a driving licence. When I politely asked to see it after a near-death experience at a roundabout, he suggested I remove myself before his hand made contact with my arse. Which is unnecessary talk in a man who fought for his country in the Viking invasions. I said to him, "You are only letting yourself down by that kind of talk, Mr Attwood."

Two minutes later

Walked up the drive to Chez Bonkers. Opened the door and yelled, "Hello, everyone, you can get out the fatted hamster, I am home!!!"

Two minutes later

No one in.

Typico.

I don't know why they ramble on so much about where I'm going and what time I will be in, when they so clearly don't give two short flying mopeds.

Kitchen
I'm starving.

Nothing in the fridge of course.

Unless you like out-of-date bean sprouts.

Four minutes later
Slightly mouldy toast, mmmmm. I think I am getting scurvy from lack of vitamin C, my hair feels tired. Perhaps Italian Luuurve Gods like the patchy-hair look in a girlfriend.

I wonder if he has left a message on the phone for me?

Five minutes later
I really wish I hadn't listened to the messages – it is a terrifying insight into the "life" I lead.

First it was some giggling pal of Mum's saying that she had met a bloke at a speed-dating night and had got to number six with him. How does she know about the snogging scale? My mum is obviously part crap mother and part seeing-ear dog.

The next message was from Josh's mum, saying, "After Josh came home with a Mohican haircut I don't think it is a good idea that he comes round to play with Libby again. I am frankly puzzled as to why she had bread knives and scissors in her bedroom. Also I cannot get the blue make-up off his eyes. I suspect it is indelible ink, which means the word BUM on his forehead will take many hours to get off."

There was a bit more rambling and moaning, but the gist is that Josh is banned from playing with my little sister Libby.

Dear *Gott in Himmel*.

And that was it. No message from the Luuurve God. It's been a week now. I wonder why he hasn't called? Has he gone off me?

Maybe I did something wrong when we last saw each other.

One minute later

But it was so vair vair gorgey porgey.

One minute later

He said, "We like each other. It will be good, Miss Georgia."

one minute later
What he didn't say was, "I will call you as soon as I get there."

one minute later
Or "I will pay your airfare to Rome, you entrancing Sex Kitty."

Ten minutes later
God, I am so bored. And my bottom still hurts from my falling-in-the-river fiasco. So I can't even sit down properly.

one minute later
I wonder if Dave the Laugh will tell Emma about our accidental number four episode. Probably not. After all, it didn't mean anything and, as he said, we are mates in a matey way. And what goes on in the woods stays in the woods.

Thirty seconds later
Hmmm. He also said in the woods that he has always really liked me. Maybe he meant that in a matey-type mate way.

one minute later
Will I tell Masimo?

One minute later

If he doesn't ring me, I won't have to make the decision. Anyway, it was only an accidental number four, verging on the number five. It could happen to anyone.

One minute later

It could happen to Masimo and his ex-girlfriend. What was her name? Gina. Yes, it might happen if, for instance, she happened to be in Rome.

One minute later

Even if she is not there, I bet he and his mates will be roaring round Rome on their scooters smiling at all the girls in their red bikinis or whatever it is they wear there.

Probably nothing. They probably go to work in the nuddy-pants because they are wild and free Pizza-a-gogo types. They don't have inhibitions like us, they just thrust their nungas forward proudly and untamed. Probably.

In my bedroom looking in the mirror

The only thing that is really thrusting itself forward proudly is my nose. Even Dave mentioned it.

One minute later

Perhaps it has grown bigger and bigger in Masimo's imagination in the week he has been away. He hasn't even got a photo of me to remind him that I am more than just a nose on legs.

Five minutes later

Perhaps because he is foreign he is a bit psychic. Perhaps he has a touch of the Mystic Meg about him and he knows about the Dave the Laugh incident.

One minute later

Jas has probably sent a message via an owl to let him know. Just because she has got the hump with me. AGAIN. About the stupid tent business.

Lying on my bed of pain
8:00 p.m.

And I mean that quite literally because my cat Angus (also known as a killing machine) is pretending my foot is a rabbit. In a sock. If I even move it slightly, he leaps on it and starts biting it.

Also, ouch and double ouch. I can't get into a comfy

position to take the pressure off my bum-oley. I think I may have actually broken something in my bottom. I don't know what there is to break, but I may have broken it. I wonder if it is swollen up?

Then I heard the *phut phut* of the mighty throbbing engine that is my vati's crap car. Carefully easing my broken bottom off the bed and slapping at Angus, I went downstairs. Angus was still clinging to my sock-rabbit-foot even though his head was bonking against the stairs.

As I got to the hall I heard the front door being kicked. Oh good, it was my delightful little sister.

"Gingey, Gingey, let me in!!! Let me in, poo sister."

Then there was squealing, like a pig was being pushed through the letter box.

Thirty seconds later

It wasn't a pig being pushed through the letter box, it was Gordy, cross-eyed son of Angus. I could see his ginger ears poking through.

Oh, bloody hell.

I said, "Libby, don't put Gordy though the letter box. I'm opening the door."

She yelled, "He laaikes it."

When I got the door open, it was to find Libby in Wellington boots and a bikini. Gordy was struggling and yowling in her little fat arms and finally squirmed free and leaped off into the garden sneezing and shaking.

Libby was laughing. "Funny pussy. *Hnk hnk.*" Then she came up to me and started hugging my knees and kissing them. In between snogging, Libby was murmuring, "I lobe my Gingey."

Mutti came up the steps in a really short dress, very tight round the nungas. So very sad. She gave me a hug, which can be quite frightening seeing her enormous basoomas looming towards your head. She said, "Hello, Gee, did you have a larf camping?"

I said, "Oh yes, it was brillopads. We made instruments out of dried beans and Herr Kamyer did impressions of crap stuff with his hands that no one could get except Jas. And, as a *pièce de résistance*, I fell in a pond and was attacked by great toasted newts."

She wasn't even listening as usual, off in her own Muttiland.

"We went to see Uncle Eddie's gig at The Ambassador last night. It was like an orgy; one of the women got so carried away she stole his feather codpiece."

Is that really the sort of thing a growing, sensitive girl should have to listen to? It was like earporn.

One minute later

I watched her bustling about making our delicious supper (i.e. opening a tin of tomato soup). She was so full of herself burbling on and on.

"Honestly, you should have been there, it was a hoot."

I said, "Ooooooh yeah, it would have been great to have been there. Really great." But she didn't get it.

Libby was still kissing my knees and giggling. She had forgotten that they were my knees; they were now just her replacement friends for Josh. But then she had a lovers' tiff with her knee-friends, biffed me on the knee quite hard and went off into the garden, yelling for Gordy.

I said, "Mum, you didn't take Libby with you to the baldy-o-gram fiasco, did you?"

"Don't be silly, Georgia, I'm not a complete fool."

I said, "Well, actually, you are as it happens."

She said, "Don't be so rude."

I said, "Where's Dad? Have you managed to shake him off at last?"

And then Vati came in. In his leather trousers. Oh, I might be sick. Not content with the horrificnosity of the trousers, he kissed me on my hair. Urgh, he had touched my hair; now I would have to wash it.

He was grinning like a loon and taking his jacket off.

"Hello, no camping injuries then. No vole bites. You didn't slip into a newt pond or anything?"

I looked at him suspiciously. I hoped he wasn't turning into Mystic Meg as well in his old age. I said, "Dad, are you wearing a woman's blouse?"

He went completely ballisticisimus. "Don't be so bloody cheeky! This is an original sixties Mod shirt. I will probably wear it when I go clubbing. Any gigs coming up?"

Mum said, "Have you heard anything from the Italian Stallion?"

Dad had his head in the fridge and I could see his enormous leather-clad bum leering at me. I had an overwhelming urge to kick it, but I wasn't whelmed because I knew he would probably ban me from going out for life.

I gave Mum my worst look and nodded over at the fridge. I needn't have worried, though, because Dad had found a Popsicle in the freezer and was as thrilled as it is possible for a fat bloke in constraining leather trousers to be. He went chomping off into the front room.

Mum was adjusting her over-the-shoulder-boulder-holder and looking at me.

I said, "What?"

And she said, "So... have you heard anything?"

I don't know why I told her, but it just came tumbling out.

"Mum, why do boys do that 'see you later' thing and then just not see you later? Even though you don't even know when later is."

"He hasn't got in touch then?"

"No."

She sat down and looked thoughtful, which was a bit alarming. She said slowly, "Hmm – well, I think it's because – they're like sort of nervous gazelles in trousers, aren't they?"

I looked at her. "Mum, are you saying that Masimo is a leaping furry animal who also plays in a band and rides a scooter? And snogs?"

She said, "He snogs, does he?"

Damn, drat, damnity dratty damn. And also *merde*. I had broken my rule about never speaking about snognosity questions with old mad people.

I said quickly, "Anyway, what do you mean about the gazelle business?"

"Well, I think that boys are more nervous than you think. He wants to make sure that you like him before he makes a big deal about it. How many days is it since he went?"

"I don't know. I haven't been counting the days actually, I'm not that sad."

She looked at me. "How many hours then?"

"One hundred and forty."

We were interrupted by Gordy and Angus both trying to get through the cat flap at once. Quickly followed by Libby.

In my bedroom
8:45 p.m.

I can hear Mum and Dad arguing downstairs because he hasn't taken the rubbish out. And never does. On and on.

I will never behave like this when I am married. Mind you, I will not be marrying a loon in tight trousers who thinks Rolf Harris is a really good artist.

Who will I be marrying at this rate? I haven't been out of my room for years and the phone hasn't rung since it was invented.

Why is no one phoning me? Not even the Ace Gang. I've been home for hours and hours. Don't they care?

The trouble with today is that everyone is so obsessed with themselves. They just have no time for me.

Five minutes later

At last, a bit of peace to contemplate my broken bum. Oh no, here they go again. They are so childish. Mum shouted out, "Bob, you know that sort of wooden thing in the bedroom, in the corner? Well, it's called a set of drawers and some people, people who are grown up and no longer have their mummy wiping their botties, well those sort of people put their clothes in the drawers. So that other people don't have to spend their precious time falling over knickers and so on."

Uh-oh. Fight, fight!!

Then I could hear him shambling into their bedroom and singing, "One little sock in the drawer, two socks in the drawer and two pairs of attractive undercrackers on the head then into the drawer, yesssss!!"

How amazing. I shouted down, "Mum, is Dad on some kind of medication? Or have his trousers cut off the circulation to his head?"

That did it. Vati hit number seven on the losing it scale (complete ditherspaz). He yelled up, "Georgia... this isn't anything to do with you!"

I said, "Oh, that's nice. I thought we were supposed to be a lovely family and do stuff together."

He just said, "Anyway, where is your sister? Is she up there with you?"

Why am I Libby's so-called nanny? Haven't I got enough trouble with my own life? I am not my sister's keeper, as Baby Jesus said. Or was it Robin Hood? I don't know. Some bloke in a skirt anyway.

I said, "No. Have you tried the airing cupboard or the cat basket?"

Five minutes later

Things have got worse. While Mum went hunting for Bibbsy, Dad unfortunately decided to check the phone messages. He heard Mum's mate's message. I could hear him tutting. And then it was Josh's mum's message.

He had the nervy spaz of all nervy spazzes, shouting and carrying on. "What is it with this family??? Why did Libby have a bread knife in her bedroom? Probably

♡ 37

because you are too busy pratting around with your so-called mates to bother looking after your children!"

That did it for Mum. She shouted back, "How dare you! They're MY children, are they? If you took some notice of them, that would be a miracle. You care more about that ridiculous bloody three-wheeled clown car."

Mum had called his car a clown car. Tee-hee.

Dad had really lost it. "That car is an antique."

I shouted, "It's not the only one."

Mum laughed, but Dad said, "Right, that's it, I'm off. Don't wait up."

Mum shouted, "Don't worry, I won't." The door slammed and there was silence.

Then there was the sound of the clown car being driven off at high speed (two miles an hour) down the driveway.

And silence again as it whirred away into the distance.

Then a little voice said, "Mummy, my bottom is stuck in the bucket."

9:30 p.m.
Dear God, what a nightmare. This has taken my mind off the oven of luuurve situation.

Libby has wedged herself into the outdoor metal bucket. We pulled her and wiggled her about but we can't get it off.

Mum said, "Go and get me some butter from the fridge. We can smear it on her and sort of slide her out."

Of course, we didn't have any butter; we had about a teaspoon of cottage cheese but Mum said it wasn't the same.

Twenty-five minutes later

In the end Mum made me go across the road and ask Mr Across the Road if we could borrow some butter. She said I could lie better.

Mr Across the Road was wearing a short nightshirt and I kept not looking anywhere below his chin. He was all nosey about the late-night butter scenario though.

"Doing a bit of baking, are you?"

I said, "Er... yes."

"It's a bit late to start, isn't it?"

I said, "Er, well, it's emergency baking. It has to be done by tomorrow."

He said, "Oh, what are you making?"

How the hell did I know? I was lying. And also the only kind of confectionery I knew were the cakes I had got from the bakery of love. The Robbie éclair, the Masimo cream horn and then I remembered the Dave the Tart scenario and quickly said, "Erm, we're making tarts. For the deaf. It's for charity."

He said, "Tarts for the deaf? That's a new one on me. I'll have to go down to the storeroom for some packets." And he ambled off.

And that is when Junior Blunder Boy and full-time twit came in. Oscar.

He looked at me and said, "Yo, wa'appen, bitch?"

What was he talking about and also what was he wearing? He had massive jeans on about fifty sizes too big for him. He had to sort of waddle about like a useless duck to keep them from falling down. And pull them up every five seconds. How spectacularly naff and sad he was. I just looked at him as he waddled over to the kitchen counter. He reached up to get a can of Coca-Cola from a shelf and momentarily forgot about his elephant jeans. They fell to his ankles. Leaving him standing there in his Thomas the Tank Engine undercrackers.

I said to him, "Oscar, you are wearing Thomas the Tank Engine undercrackers. I know this because, believe it or not, your trousers have fallen off."

He said, "Yes man, me mean to do that. Be cool, it is righteous." And he shuffled off, still with the trousers round his ankles.

I will never, ever tire of the sheer bonkerosity of boydom.

11:00 p.m.

It took us nearly half an hour to get Mr Bucket off Libby. We greased as much of her bottom as we could reach, like a little suckling pig. Eventually we cut through the top of her panties and managed to make a bit of leeway and free the bum-oley.

For some toddlers, being greased up and pulled by brute force out of a metal bucket might have been a traumatic experience. But then not all toddlers are insane. Libby laughed and sang through the whole episode, amusing herself by gobbling stray bits of butter and smearing other bits on my head. Oh, how I joined in the merry times. Not.

In addition, Gordy and Angus lolloped in to lick at the leftover butter on her botty. Soooo disgusting. Libby was shouting, "They is ticklin me!!! Heggy heggy ho!!!"

Back in bed

It is like the botty casualty department in here. My bottom, which I have had no time to attend to, is being supported by Libby's swimming ring and I have a buttered-up child rammed in next to me.

Also, have I got a boyfriend or not?

Midnight

And I am still thinking about the Dave the Laugh accidental snogging in the forest incident.

12:10 a.m.

Perhaps this is God's little way of saying, "She who lives by the red bottom gets to lie in a rubber ring."

once more into the huffmobile

Monday August 1st

8:00 a.m.
Oww oww and double owww!! I think my botty has taken a turn for the worse. I wonder if it is swollen up?

Looking in the mirror
It does look a bit on the swollen side. Oh marvellous. I will have to ask Jas if I can borrow some of her enormous winter pants. She will have got them out of her winter store by now. She starts ironing her school pants about a month before we are forced back to Stalag 14. Which reminds me, we only

 43

have about four weeks of holiday left. *Sacré bleu* and *merde*.

Libby has already scarpered off to get ready for nursery, so I can just have a little dolly daydream about snogging the Luuurve God. If I make a mental picture of us snogging, I might attract him to me through the psychic ethery stuff.

Ten minutes later

I can hear the postman coming up the drive. Ah, the postie. It's a lovely job being a postie; you see it in all ye olde films that ye olde parents watch. Mr Postie coming up the drive with a cheery whistle and a handful of exciting letters for the family. A "Good morning, ma'am" to the mistress of the house and then—

"I've got a bloody stick, you furry freak, and I'm not afraid to use it!!!"

Charming. Utterly, utterly charming.

I looked out of the window. Angus was sitting on the dustbin showing off to Naomi, his mad Burmese girlfriend and slag, by taunting the postie – hissing and doing pretend biffing, sticking his claws in and out. The postie had to get by the dustbin to get to the door and he was waving a big stick about in Angus's direction. Angus loves a stick. The larger the better. He lay down and started purring so loudly I could

44

hear it in my bedroom. I don't know why he loves sticks so much, but he does. Almost as much as he loves cars.

He thinks cars are like giant stupid mice on wheels. That he can chase after.

He brought a stick home the other day that was so big, it took him half an hour to figure out how to get it through the cat flap. He did it, though, because he is top cat.

Two minutes later

It was the same with the ginormous dead pigeon. Angus backed his way through the cat flap dragging the feet first, and then Gordy heave-hoed the head bit through.

It was an amazing double act. Father and son were very impressed with themselves. Although slightly covered in feathers. They even arranged the pigeon so that it was looking towards the door and propped up so Mum could get the full benefit when she came in.

She did get the full benefit and went ballistic, jumping on a chair and screaming etc. Angus and Gordy and the dead pigeon all looked at her.

"Bloody murdering furry thugs!!!" she yelled.

I said, "Look, you are really hurting their feelings."

And then she threw the washing-up bowl at me. That is the kind of mothering I have to put up with.

One minute later

The postie has bravely got past Angus and disappeared from view as he posts our letters through the letter box. Angus has disappeared as well. Oh, I know what he is doing!

He is doing his vair vair amusing trick of lurking in the top of the hedge to leap down on the postie's head as he passes by. Tee-hee. Happy days. I wish I was a cat. At least I would get fed now and again.

I wouldn't be quite so keen on all the bum-oley licking. Although as mine is so swollen now, it would probably be easier to reach.

Mum yelled up, "Gee, come down and have brekkie and say goodbye to your family."

I said, "Have I still got one? I thought that Father had left us and would never be back. That is what he promised."

Dad yelled up, "You think you are so bloody funny, but you won't when I don't give you your ten-quid pocket money. Nothing to spend on your eyeliner or nit cream or whatever else it is that you plaster yourself with."

Nit cream? Has he finally snapped?

Mum said, "Stop it, you two. Oooh look, here is a foreign postcard addressed to Georgia – I wonder who it's from?"

Oh my giddy god's pyjamas!!! I leaped downstairs, putting the pain of my bottom behind me. Tee-hee. Oh brilliant, my brain has gone into hysterical clown mode.

Thirty seconds later

Dad had the postcard in his hand and was reading it!!! Noooooo!

He was saying in a really crap Pizza-a-gogo accent, "*Ciao, Georgia, it is smee.*"

I tried to get the postcard from him. "Dad, that is private property addressed to me. If it doesn't say 'to some mad fat bloke', it isn't yours."

Dad just went on reading it. "I am, how you say, hair in Roma wive my family."

Finally I ripped it out of his hand and took it upstairs.

Mum said, "You are mean, Bob. You know what she is like."

Dad said, "Yes, I do. She's insane like all the other bloody women in this family. Hang on a minute... what the hell happened to my car-washing bucket?"

Mum said, "We had to hit it with a hammer in the end. Libby got her bottom stuck in it."

Dad said, "I rest my case."

In my room
Oh God, I am sooooo excited, my eyes have gone cross-eyed. What does it say?

Twenty seconds later

> Ciao, Georgia,
>
> It is smee. I am, how you say, hair in Roma wive my family. I am hot. (You don't have to tell me that, mate.) I am playing fun. Are you playing fun? I miss I you me.
>
> I call on the telefono on Tuesday for you.
>
> Ciao, bellissima, Masimo xxx

An hour later
After about three thousand years and a half, the Swiss Family Mad all crashed off to ruin other people's lives and I could get on the old blower.

I nearly dialled Wise Woman of the Forest before I remembered that she had practically called me the Whore of Babylon. She is so full of suspicionosity. And annoyingnosity. How dare she suggest in front of everyone that I had been up to hanky-panky and rudey-dudeys with Dave the Laugh? She knows very well that I am going out with a Luuurve God. Who is a) hot and b) playing fun.

What in the name of arse does "playing fun" mean?

I must consult with my gang.

But not her.

I am *ignorez-vous*ing her with a firm hand and it serves her right. I hope she realises that I am *ignorez-vous*ing her, otherwise it's all a bit pointless.

Two minutes later

I may have to call her and let her know I am *ignorez-vous*ing her, as she can be a bit on the dense side.

Phoned Jas.

Her mum answered. "Hello, Georgia. Gosh, you had a fabulous time camping, didn't you? Jas said you sang and played games till all hours."

I said, "Er yes…"

"You had a great time, I bet."

"Er yes, it was very, erm, campey."

"Good. I'll just call Jas, dear. I think she's in her bedroom dusting and rearranging her owls and so on."

You couldn't really write it, could you? If I wrote a book and I said: "I've got a mate who dusts her collection of stuffed owls and follows greater toasted newts about," people would say: "I'm not reading that sort of stupid exaggeration. Next thing you know, someone will say they went to a party dressed as a stuffed olive. Or accidentally snogged three boyfriends at once." Hang on a minute, everything has gone a bit *déjà vu*-ish.

Jas came on the phone. "Yes."

"Jas, it is me, the Whore of Babylon, but I am preparing myself to forgive you."

"What are you forgiving me for?"

"Because you are a naughty pally saying things about me being selfish and lax and having a million boyfriends."

Jas said, "It's up to you how many boyfriends you have. I am not my brother's keeper."

"Jas, I know you aren't. You haven't got a brother."

"I mean you."

"I haven't got a brother either, thank the Lord. I do,

however, have an insane sister, who by the way is now probably going to be done for TBH."

"You mean GBH – grievous bodily harm."

"No, I mean TBH. Toddler bodily harm. Josh's mum has complained about her and she is suspended from nursery school. She is staying with Grandfarty and he is looking after her. She is the first person in our family to get a restraining order besides Grandad."

Jas was not what you would call full of sympatheticnosity.

"I don't think she will be the last person in your family to get a restraining order, Georgia. I am a bit busy actually."

"Jas, please don't have Mrs Hump with me. I need you, my dearest little pally wally. Pleasey please, be frendy wendys. Double please with knobs. And a tiny little knoblet. And—"

"All right, all right, stop going on."

She deffo had the minor hump, but it was only four on the having-the-hump scale. (cold-shoulderosity work).

"Jas, come on. Remember the laugh we had when we all snuck off to the boys' tent? And I came and told you that Tom was there, didn't I? Even though you were singing 'Ging Gang Gooly'."

"Well, yes, but—"

"I displayed magnanimosity, which isn't something everyone can say. But I did it because I luuurve you. A LOT."

"OK, don't go on."

"You are not ashamed of our luuurve, are you, Jas?"

"Look, shut up. People might hear."

"What do you mean, the people who live in the telephone?"

"NO, I mean, anyway, what's happened?"

"I've got a postcard from Masimo and we have to call an extraordinary general meeting of the Ace Gang."

"Oh no."

"Oh yes."

In the park
2:00 p.m.

Naaaice and sunny. I wore my denim miniskirt and halter neck and some groovy sandals. I will have to do something with my legs, though, because they give me the droop, they are so pale. Rosie had some eye-catching shorts on; they had pictures of Viking helmets all over them. She said, "Sven had them specially printed in my honour. Groovy, aren't they?"

I said, "That is one word for them."

Rosie said, "Sven has got his first dj-ing job next weekend and I am going to be his groupie. You all have to come."

Ten minutes later

We settled down in the shade underneath the big chestnut tree by the swings. The bees were singing and the birds a-buzzing, dogs scampering around, people eating ice creams, toddlers sticking ice creams in their eyes by mistake etc. A lovely, lovely summer afternoon, ideal to sort out the game of luuurve.

We had just passed round the chuddie and decided for Ellen where she should sit after about eight minutes of: "Well, erm, I should sit in the shade really, don't you think, because of the ultraviolet, but, erm, what about, erm, not like getting the sun and then like maybe not getting enough vitamin D because that would be, like, not great. Or something."

Finally she sat with her top part in the shade and her legs sticking in the sun because we told her no one had ever got cancer of the knees. Which might or might not be true, but sometimes (in fact, very often, in my experience) lying is the best policy. Especially if you can't be arsed talking about something boring any more.

One minute later

I don't know why I bother lying because Ellen has gone off to the loos to run her wrists under cold water so she doesn't get sunstroke of the arms.

Jas still hasn't turned up. I wonder if she has progressed to number six on the hump scale and is doing pretend deafnosity?

Thirty seconds later

The Ace Gang started talking about the camping trip and sneaking out to see the lads at night.

Mabs said, "I had a go at snogging with Edward."

Jools said, "What was it like?"

Mabs chewed and popped and said, "Quite groovy. We did four and then a spot of five."

I said, "Oh, so *you* missed out four and a half as well. I said I thought it was a WUBBISH idea that Mrs Newt Knickers came up with. Who apart from her and Tom would do hand snogging?"

Mabs said, "What do you mean 'as well'?"

I said, "What do you mean 'What do you mean as well?'"

Mabs put her face really close to mine. "Georgia, you said,

and forgive me if I'm right, 'Oh, so you missed out four and a half as well.' Which means, 'Oh, so you missed out four and a half as well AS ME.' Meaning you must have missed out four and a half with someone. The only someone around was Dave the Laugh."

Uh-oh, my red-herringnosity skills were letting me down.

Mabs was going on and on like Jas's little helper. "So what did you get up to with Dave the Laugh by the river?"

I said in a casualosity-at-all-times sort of way, "Ah well, I'm glad you asked me that. Because suspicionosity is the enemy of friendshipnosity. The simple truth is that Dave and I were playing, erm, tig. Yes, and I accidentally fell in a stream and then I went back to my tent because I was, er, wet."

Rosie said, "You and Dave were playing tig. I see. One moment. I must give this some serious thought. Luckily I have my pipe."

Oh no.

Two minutes later

Good Lord, I am being interrogated by Inspector Bonkers of the Yard.

The inspector (i.e. Rosie with her pipe and beard on)

continued, "You expect us to believe that you and Dave the Laugh gambolled around the woods playing a little game of tig?"

I said, "Yes."

Rosie said, "You are, it has to be said, my little chumlet, even dimmer than you look."

Ellen came back then, just in the knickers of time. I smiled at her and said in a lighthearted but menacing way, "You haven't told us about Declan. It is Ace Gang rules that we do sharesies about snogging."

Rosie and Mabs raised their eyebrows at me, but I *ignorez-vous*ed them.

Ellen heaved herself into her Dithermobile and said, "Well, Declan showed, well, he showed me something and—"

Inspector Bonkers of the Yard winked, sucked on her pipe and went, "Ay ay."

Ellen went even redder and more dithery.

"No, I mean, it was his Swiss Army knife."

Inspector Bonkers got out a pretend notebook. "All right. So you looked at his knife and then did you snog?"

Ellen said, "Well, when we were, like, leaving to go back to camp – he gave me a number three and then—"

56

"Then quickly went on to number four."

"Well, no, he..."

"He missed out number four and went straight for the nungas?"

"No, well, he – he, like, he said, he said, 'See you later.'"

Oh dear God, we were once more in the land of S'later. Will we never be free?

One minute later

But at least it stopped anyone going on about the Dave the Laugh fiasco.

One minute later

Jas turned up. She looked quite nice actually, if you like that mad fringey look. She said, "I was just talking to Tom on the phone. He's playing footie this arvie with the lads. He's got some new boots."

I said, "No!! Honestly!"

And she gave me a huffty look. I don't want to have more rambling lectures from her, so I went and gave her a hug and a piece of chuddie.

Anyway, we had just settled down and I'd got out my

postcard from Masimo to show the gang, when Jools said, "Oh God, Blunder Boys alert!"

They were shuffling about by the bushes at the far end of the swing park. Mark Big Gob was absent, probably carrying his tiny girlfriend around somewhere. Junior Blunder Boy was with them though. I noticed he had a belt round his elephant jeans. So now he didn't look like a twit any more. He looked like a twit with a belt on.

Mabs said, "Don't look at them and they'll get bored."

I said, "Can we get back to the matter I hold in my hand?"

Rosie went, "Oo-er."

I gave her my worst look and went on, "What do you think 'I am playing fun' means?"

Ellen said, "Well, erm, I don't know but you know, well – well, you know when a boy says 'See you later', well, like when Declan said 'See you later' and that was, like, three days ago now. So, er, this is, like, later, isn't it? Or something. And he hasn't, like, seen me."

Even though we were actually officially having the official Ace Gang meeting officially for me (as I had officially called it), I did feel quite sorry for Ellen. And also it has to be said it would be a bloody relief if she did get off with Declan.

Then she would leave Dave the Laugh alone.

Not that it is any of my business whether she leaves Dave the Laugh alone or not.

I mean, he has a girlfriend anyway.

Probably.

Unless he has told her about the accidental snogging and she is even now taking kickboxing lessons for when she next sees me.

Anyway, shut up, brain. He has got a girlfriend, which is good because so have I.

Well, not a girlfriend exactly, but an Italian person.

Who incidentally does not have a handbag.

Or a sports bra.

Whatever Dave the so-called Laugh might say. Why is Dave the Laugh sneaking about in my brain???

Jools said to Ellen, "Maybe he's a bit shy."

Ellen said, "Yes, but he, I mean, he showed me his Swiss Army knife."

I looked at her. What is the right response to that? I said, "Well, maybe he is a bit backward then?"

Ellen looked like she was going to cry. Oh Blimey O'Reilly's Y-fronts, if she starts blubbing, I'll never get round to talking about the Italian Stallion.

I said quickly, "I know... Jas can ask Tom to get Declan and the lads to come along to Sven's gig, and hopefully that will be a good excuse for him to get his knife out again (oo-er) and everything will be tickety-boo and so on."

Ellen looked a bit cheered up.

I said, "Now, shall we get back to the official meeting? What do you think 'I am playing fun' means?" And that is when an elastic band hit me on the cheek.

"Owww, bloody owww!!!"

Amazingly, not content with being complete losers, tossers and spoons, the Blunder Boys were flicking rubber bands at us from behind our tree. And then hiding behind it as if we wouldn't know where they were. Like the Invisible Twits. Not.

I got up and went behind the tree where they were all larding about, puffing smoke from fags and hitching their trousers up. Dear God. I said to one of the speccy genks, "What is it you want?"

And he said, "Show us your nungas."

They all started snorting and saying, "Yeah, get them out for the lads."

Rosie came up behind me and loomed over them. She is not small. She said, "OK, that's a good plan. We'll show you our nungas, but first of all we need to see your trouser snakes, to check that all is in order."

Ellen and Jools and Mabs and even Woodland Jas came and ganged up in front of them.

I said, "Come on, lads, drop the old trouser-snake holders."

They started backing off, holding on to their trousers.

Jools said, "Are you a bit shy? Shall we help you?"

They started walking really quickly backwards as we kept walking. Then they just took off and got over the fence at the back of the park.

Twelve minutes later

The Ace Gang wisdomosity is that "I am playing fun" and "Are you playing fun?" roughly translated into Billy Shakespeare language is "I am having a nice time but am missing you. Are you having a nice time but missing me?"

Which is nice.

So all should be smoothy friendly friendly, except that there is always a Jas in the manger.

After about two hours of talking about it, we were all going home and I just innocently said, "So what do you think I should wear when he phones up?"

And Jas immediately climbed into the huffmobile for no apparent reason. She was all red and flicking her fringe around like it was a fringe-ometer.

"Why is it always like this with you, Georgia? Why don't you just say and do normal stuff? For instance, if Tom wanted me to go to the nature reserve with him he would say, 'Jas, do you want to go to the nature reserve with me? There is a conservation day and we could clear some of the canalside of weeds.'

"And I would say, 'Yes, that would be fab, Tom.' Simple pimple, not stupidity and guessing what 'playing fun' means and what to wear on the phone."

What was she rambling on about now?

I said, "Jas are the painters in, because I think you are being just a tad more mentally unstable than normal."

She really had lost her cheese now, because she shouted at me, "Look, I haven't got any sun protector on and I am almost bound to get peely peely now thanks to you going on. And the short and short of it is that HE IS CALLING YOU TOMORROW AND YOU CAN ASK HIM WHAT HE MEANS!!!" And she stormed off.

Blimey. We all looked at one another.

I said, "I think it's owl trouble."

In bed

What am I going to wear for the phone call though? I wish I wasn't so pale; I think people can tell if you are a bit tanned. Even down the phone. I bet I can tell immediately if he has a nice tan.

Two minutes later

Actually, if he is tanned I think I might faint. I can't stand him being much more gorgey than he already is.

Five minutes later

Should I prepare a speech? Or at least a normal conversation. With some handy topics in case I mislay my brain or it decides to go on an expedition to Outer Loonolia.

One minute later

So let's see, what have I done lately?

Loads of stuff.

Five minutes later

I don't think I will mention Miss Wilson exposing herself to Herr Kamyer.

Two minutes later
Or breaking my bum-oley in the river.

Four minutes later
In fact, perhaps it's better to leave the whole camping fiasco to one side. I will only have Dave the Laugh popping into my brain. I will stick to lighthearted banter.

   Should I tell him about the tarts for the deaf episode?

Three minutes later
Or Junior Blunder Boy's Thomas the Tank Engine undercrackers?

Two minutes later
None of it sounds that normal, to be frank. I will stick to world affairs and art.

Two minutes later
I could ask him what he thinks about the foreign exchange rate. Well, I could if I knew what it meant.

one minute later

Where is Rome anyway? Is it in the boot bit of Italy? Or is Spain the booty bit?

I'm really worried about tomorrow now. I will never sleep and then I will have big dark rings under my eyes and...

zzzzzzzzzzzzzzz.

Tuesday August 2nd
9:30 a.m.

I was just having a dream about being in Rome with the Luuurve God. I had a cloak on and Masimo said, "So, *cara,* what have you come to the fancy-dress party as?" And I dropped the cloak and said, "A fried egg."

The phone rang and I practically broke my neck tripping over Angus and Gordy, who just emerged from the shadows.

I couldn't say anything because I was so nervous.

Then I heard Grandad say, "Hello, hello, speak up."

I said, "Grandad, I haven't said anything yet."

He was in full-Grandad mode. "You'll like this: what do pigs use if they hurt themselves? Ay ay??? Oinkment. Do you get it, do you see??? Oinkment!!! Oh, I make myself laugh. Are you courting yet? You should be – there's nothing like a bit of snogging to perk you up."

Oh dear God, my grandvati was talking about snogging.

Now I have finally experienced every kind of porn. This is mouldyporn.

Two minutes later

I managed to get him off the phone by saying good morning to Libby (she purred back), and promising to visit and have a game of hide-and-seek with him and the other residents. I don't mind that so much, as when it is my turn to hide I just go to the shops and then come back half an hour later and get in a cupboard. It keeps them happy for hours.

I do love my grandad though. He is one of the most cheerful people I know and now he is going to have Maisie as his new knitted wife. Aaaahhh.

Mum was wandering around in the kitchen like Madame Zozo of, erm, Zozoland. In a semi-see-through nightie. It's her day off and she looked like she might settle in for hours. I must get rid of her.

I said in an interested and lighthearted fashion, "What

time are you going out? In a minute or two? To make the best of the day?"

She sat down, actually resting her basoomas on the tabletop, presumably because she was already tired of lugging them about. Please save me from the enormous-jug gene.

She said, "I thought you and I could go out and do something groovy together."

Groovy?

I said, "Mum, are you mad because I tell you this for free a) I am not going out with you and b) the same with knobs on."

Mum said, "Hahaha, that worried you. Are you having a bit of a nervy spazmarama attack about Masimo ringing you?"

I was truly shocked. "Mum, it is not a nervy spazmarama, it is a spaz attack, which is number six on the losing it scale – hang on a minute. How do you know about a spaz attack anyway? Have you been snooping through my private drawers?"

She didn't bother to reply because she was too busy eating jam with a spoon out of the jar. She will get so fat that she will get trapped in Dad's clown car and have to drive endlessly up and down our driveway begging for snacks from passers-by. Good.

When she stopped chomping, she said, "Me and my mates

have loads of sayings and stuff. We have a real laugh. It's not just you and your mates, you know. I have a life."

I tried not to laugh.

"In aquarobics the other day Fiona laughed so much at the instructor's choice of music that she weed herself in the pool. When she told me I nearly drowned. We had to all leave the class and I don't think we can go back."

She was hiccuping and giggling like a twerp. Is it any wonder that I find myself in trouble with boys when I have this sort of thing as my example?

I left the kitchen with a dignitosity-at-all-times sort of walk. I have a call from the cakeshop of luuurve to think about.

Back in my bedroom
Ten minutes later

What shall I wear, what shall I wear? I tell you this, I'm not going to wear anything yellow after the fried egg dream.

I could wear my bikini. My red one with the dots on it. They tend to wear red bikinis all the time the Italian girls, probably even if they work in banks and cafes and so on. Maybe not for nursing though; it might not be hygienic. My mum said that when she had an Italian boyfriend she was on the beach and this bloke rode up on a motorbike. And this girl who just had on the bottoms of a bikini and some really high heels came jogging up. She got on the back of the bike, lit a fag and they roared off with her nunga-nungas flying.

Back in the kitchen
9:45 a.m.
Why won't Mum go out? I have my bikini on underneath my ordinary clothes ready to rip off when the phone rings.

Five minutes later
She is just rambling on and on about herself. I already know more than I want to know about her.

9:55 a.m.
Oh nooooooo. Now she is talking about "feelings" and "relationships" and what is worse is, it's not even my feelings or relationships, it's hers!!! How horrific.

She says she feels that she doesn't share many interests with Dad.

I said, "Well, who does?"

She didn't even hear me, she just went on and on. "I think when I met him I was a different person and now I've changed."

10:10 a.m.
The Luuurve God is going to phone any minute and she will still be here.

Mum said, "I don't blame him, but people do change and want different things."

I said quickly, "Yeah, yeah, you're so right. I think you need a change – a change of, er, scenery. You need to go out into the sunshine and meet your mates and ask them what they feel. Maybe go for a slap-up meal. You've only had a pound or two of jam today, you'll be peckish. Go for a pizza and maybe have some *vino tinto* because you know what they say about *vino* in Latin. *In vino hairy arse.* Just give yourself space."

"Do you think so? Just enjoy myself and don't feel guilty?"

I nodded like billio.

Fifteen minutes later
Thank the Lord, Baby Jesus and all his cohorts. She's gone. All tarted up. It is so typically selfish of her to have a midlife crisis when I am expecting a phone call.

Half an hour later

Oh, I am so full of tensionosity. I haven't been able to eat anything apart from oven chips. With mayo and tommy sauce. And a choc ice.

Perhaps some popcorn would be good for me. It's practically health food really. In fact, don't hamsters eat it? And they are as healthy as anything. Running round and round in those little wheels for no reason, dashing up and down ladders. Ringing bells etc.

Shut up, brain! I am giving you a final warning.

Twenty minutes later

I tell you this, never cook popcorn. I don't know what happened, but I did what it said on the packet, chucked it into some hot oil in a pan and it just sort of exploded everywhere. How do you get popcorn out of light fittings?

And your hair?

And nose?

And bikini bottoms?

Angus has just done that cat thing. You know, the high-speed slink across the room with the belly nearly touching the ground. Why do they do that? Why?

Two minutes later

Now he is doing fridge staring.

Ring ring.

Ohmygiddygod. The phone. I bet all my lip gloss has disappeared. But if I go and reapply, he might ring off. Oh good, I was at number nine on the ditherspaz scale already.

I smiled as I said in my deepest voice, "Hello?"

"Georgia, have you come over all transsexual? Has he phoned yet?"

"No, he hasn't, Jas. Not that you really care."

"Yes, I do, otherwise why would I phone up to ask you whether he'd phoned you yet?"

"I don't know."

"Well, there you are then."

"You might have called just to be glad he hasn't called, knowing you."

"Well, I didn't."

"Oh, OK, thanks. Goodbye now."

"Don't you want to talk to me?"

"Er, well, not just now, Jas."

"Oh."

"I'm putting the phone down now."

72

There was a sort of a sobbing noise. Then a trembly little voice said, "Tom and I had our first row last night."

Oh for heaven's bloody sake.

I said, "What happened? Did he diss one of your owls?"

She was gulping and her voice was all trembly. "No, but he said, he said, what did I think about him going to uni in Hamburger-a-gogo land. And I said I didn't really want to go to Hamburger-a-gogo land, I would rather go to York. And he said that might be a good idea."

What is this, *EastEnders*?

Thirty minutes later

Good Lord. I think I know everything that is in Jas's head now and I tell you this for free, I wish I didn't.

Tom thinks they should go to separate unis or something so that they can be sure that they are made for each other. I did say to Jas, "Well, you can safely let him go. What other fool is he going to find to go vole hunting with him?"

But it didn't seem to cheer her up as such.

In the end I've said I'll go round to hers later after the Luuurve God has called.

God help us one and all.

one hour later

I am now officially going mad.

Phone rang

I said, "Yes! What is it?"

And then I heard his voice. "*Ciao*, er, is please Georgia there?"

It was him!!! Praise God and his enormous beard!!

I took a big breath and said, "Hello, yes, Georgia Nicolson speaking."

Blimey, why am I suddenly speaking like the queen?

Masimo laughed. "*Ciao ciao*, Georgia!! *Bellissima!!!* It is you! *Un momento per favore.*"

Then I head him speaking off the telephone and laughing, and there were other voices and then loud smacking noises like kissing.

Maybe it was kissing.

Was he actually snogging someone else while he was talking to me? That seemed very lax, even for the Pizza-a-gogo types.

Then suddenly he was back talking to me again. "Oh, *cara*, *mi scusi*, my brothers, my family, they are all going to the beach – later, when it is night we are having how you say in English – a bum-fire?"

74

A bum-fire? That seemed a bit mean. Setting people's bums on fire. But perhaps that is the old Roman ways emerging again.

Then he was laughing. "You are not saying anything. I have this wrong, no?"

I said, "*Sì.*" And we both laughed. It was marvy speaking in different languages.

He said, "Have you missed me?"

And I said, "Oh, *muchos* and a half."

He laughed again. We were laughing and laughing.

"Me too. How was your camping?"

Uh-oh. The forbidden topic. I must remember my rule about not saying anything and get things back to world politics and so on as soon as possible. I said, "Oh, it was pretty crappio."

He said, "Tell me something from it."

"Well, you know, not much happened. Erm, Nauseating P. Green fell into the so-called toilets and it fell down and Miss Wilson was in the nuddy-pants having a shower with her soap on a rope. And then later Herr Kamyer sat on her knee and that was all that happened."

He said, "I have, how you would say, the mad girlfriend."

Ooooh, he had called me his mad girlfriend. How cool was that?

We talked for ages. Well, I said stuff and he asked me what it meant mostly. I wish I could speak more Pizza-a-gogo-ese; it's more difficult speaking to someone on the phone anyway because you can't see their face. And then he asked me when I am coming over to see him.

Good point, well made.

I haven't even asked my parents about the 500 squids I will need. If they would stop banging on about themselves, I might get a chance to ask. I didn't like to say that I didn't have any money, so I just said, "I think, probably in two, *due* weeks."

He said, "Ah, that is long. I wish you were here and then we could again, what do you say – snog. And I could touch you and feel your mouth on mine. And look into your lovely face. I was thinking about your beautiful eyes and I think they are so lovely, it makes my heart melt."

Crikey, he had turned into Billy Shakespeare. Or Billio Shakespeario, who wrote the famous Italian plays *MacUselessio* and *King Leario*.

Shut up, brain. Now this minutio. Stoppio, nowio. It still wouldn't stop it (io).

I was quite literally tripping around on a cloud of luuurve. Sadly, the four pints of Coke I had to keep me going before he phoned now wanted to come out and join me.

I tried pressing my bottom against the stool but sooner or later something was going to give. I needed to go to the tarts' wardrobe vair vair badly. But because my vati was too mean to get a modern phone that you could walk about with I was stuck. I didn't want to say, "Oh, 'scuse me, I have to go to the piddly-diddly department" because that would start another one of those international incidents. So I said, "Oh no, someone is at the door. Can you just hang on for a mo?"

He said, "*Sì, cara*, I wait."

And then weirdly the doorbell did ring. How freaky-deaky is that? I wonder who it was. Well, whoever it was, they weren't coming in. I nipped into the tarts' wardrobe. Then the shouting began.

"Georgia, come on, open the door! We know you are in there."

It was Grandad. And he wasn't alone. I could hear Libby and Maisie. Dear God.

I couldn't keep them out for long because they would probably start knitting a rope ladder and get through my bedroom window. Perhaps I could persuade them to go away.

There was a bit of a silence and then Grandad said, "We've

got snacks," and he posted a sandwich through the letter box. I think it was spam.

I went back to the telephone. "Masimo, I have to go now. My grandad is posting sandwiches through the letter box.

He laughed. But he laughed alone. Then he said, "Phone me when you can. The *telefono* is Roma 75556666121." He did kissing stuff down the phone and then he was gone.

I didn't even remember to say when shall we speak again or anything because I was so flustered by the elderly loons. And I wanted to write the number down before I forgot it.

Five minutes later
People will not believe this, I know, but Maisie has knitted Libby a miniskirt and matching beret for her bridesmaid's outfit.

An hour later
They have gone, thank the Lord.

Four minutes later
Hearing Masimo's voice has made everything simple for me *vis-à-vis* the General Horn, ad-hoc red-bottomosity etc.

I am putting the accidental snogging scenario with Dave

the Laugh into a snogging cupboard at the back of my brainbox. A snogging cupboard that I will never be going into again. I have locked the door and thrown away the key.

Well, I didn't throw it away actually, but I have put it somewhere that I will never be able to find again.

One minute later
The snogging cupboard is in fact next to another cupboard that has got other discarded boy stuff in it. Like the Mark Big Gob stuff. The resting his hand on my nunga-nunga episode, for instance. Which I have also completely forgotten about and will never remember.

One minute later
That cupboard has also got the snogging Whelk Boy fiasco in it. Erlack a pongoes.

One minute later
And that cupboard is next to the set of drawers that has pictures of Robbie the original Sex God in it. Funny I haven't heard anything from him since I sort of dumped him. I hope

he is not on the rack of love. Although that would be a first. Usually it is me that is on the rack of love.

Thirty seconds later
I'll just close the drawer now.

Ten seconds later
I wonder if Robbie has got the megahump with me? I daren't ask Tom. Especially as he might be Mr Ex-Hunky.

One minute later
I hope Robbie is not too sad without me. I don't like making boys cry. Although to be frank I would rather they were crying than me.

Life can be cruel.

Especially if you are vair vair sensitive like I am.

Two minutes later
I don't know what to do with myself now. I am full of excitementosity. And tensionosity. And just a hint of confusiosity.

one minute later

Maybe I should fill in time by learning some Pizza-a-gogo-ese. For when I go over. Only being able to say *cappuccino* is going to wear a bit thin after a few days.

Masimo said he was off to some party tonight in Rome.

Five minutes later

Should he be out having fun while I am hanging about like a monk in a monkhouse? That is the drawback to being the girlfriend of a rock legend, you have to hang around a lot.

I may be driven to going round to listen to Wild Woman of the Forest ramble on about Hunky.

On the way round to Jas's

If I am nice to her, she may smash open her secret piggy bank and give me spondulies to go to my beloved.

Or else I could just steal the piggy.

Round at Jas's

Both her little eyes were swollen up. I put my arm around her and said, "Jas, I have found that when you are troubled, it is often better to think of others rather than yourself. I think you would feel much better if you got me some milky coffee and Jammy Dodgers and I told you all about me."

I had only just started when we were interrupted by Jas's mum saying there was a phone call from Rosie for Jas. Did she want to take it on her phone in the bedroom?

Jas and I each listened on an extension. I was nestled up among the Owl Folk and Jas was in her mum and dad's bedroom on the other extension.

Every time I ask for an extension and so on, Dad has a complete nervy spaz saying rubbish stuff like, "Why don't you just have a phone glued to your head?" And so on.

I am not surprised that Mum says she doesn't share many interests with him. What I am surprised about is that she shares any.

Ro Ro said, "*Bonjour*, groovers. I have had *la bonne* idea. Don't you think it would be groovy and a laugh for us to work out some backing dances for Sven's gig?

I said, "*Mais oui*, that would be *beau regarde* and also *magnifique* and possibly groovy."

Jas said, "Well, as long as they are not silly."

Rosie and I laughed, then I said, "We could have a Nordic

theme. We have many Viking dances in our repertoire: the Viking disco inferno, the bison dance. We could make up another one."

Rosie said, "Yeah, grooveyard, we could have furry miniskirts and ear muffs."

Home again
9:00 p.m.

I have cheered Jas up and told her we will think of a plan *vis-à-vis* Tom.

I didn't mention the piggy bank, but I think it is on the shelf near her bed. Behind her mollusc collection.

9:19 p.m.

I don't know why I didn't realise I was born for the stage before. It is blindingly obvious even to a blind man on blind tablets that I am a backing dancer. That will be my career. I will travel with the band giving the world the benefit of my Viking disco inferno dance and so on. And it is very convenient romance-wise because with Masimo as the lead singer of the Stiff Dylans and me as backing dancer, we can travel the globe of luuurve.

The turbulent washing machine of luuurve

Friday August 5th
Early Evening

Masimo hasn't called again. Officially it's my turn to call him on the number he gave me. That is what I would do if he was a girl, which he clearly isn't, even if Dave says he is.

Shut up about Dave.

I feel a bit shy about calling Masimo. In one of my mum's mags it said, "Be a teaser, not a pleaser." And it said you should never ring a boy; they should always ring you. So essentially, I am once more thrashing about in the washing machine of luuurve.

Oooh, what shall I do? Maybe I should send him a postcard.

Five minutes later
But if I go out and buy a postcard, he might ring while I'm out. I wonder if Mum has one lurking about in her drawers. Oo-er.

In Mum's bedroom
Honestly, this house is like living in a tart's handbag. I've found a card but it is of a girl walking by with huge nunga-nungas and a bloke on a veg stand holding two melons in front of his chest. The caption is "Phwoar, what a lovely pair of melons!" What is the matter with my parents?

Two minutes later
But even if I did manage to send a card, when would I say I was coming? I still haven't managed to steer the conversation around to Mutti and Vati giving me the spondulies for my trip.

One minute later
However, I have more than romance on my mind. Masimo will have to understand that my career comes first

sometimes. There is a rehearsal round at Rosie's tonight for our planned disco inferno extravaganza, so I'd better get my dance tights out.

Sunday August 7th

Waited for the postie at the gate yesterday, but he didn't have any letters for me. I asked him if he was hiding my mail, but he didn't even bother to reply.

More damned rehearsals for Sven's dj-ing night today. I am so vair vair tired. I am a slave to my art.

9:45 p.m.

I am quite tuckered out with dancing. Even though it is still practically the afternoon, I may as well go to bed.

In bed

Sven turned up at Rosie's while we were there and snogged the pants off her (oo-er).

We all felt like a basket of goosegogs.

In fact, when we were walking home, Jas said, "I felt a bit jealous."

I tutted. But actually I felt a bit jealous as well.

9:50 p.m.

The door slammed and I heard Vati come in. Accompanied by Uncle Eddie, a.k.a. the baldy-o-gram since he took up taking his clothes off for women. They pay him to do it, that is the weird thing.

Dad yelled, "The vati and the baldy-o-gram are home, sensation seekers!"

Ten minutes later

I can hear the sound of sizzling from the kitchen and the cats are going bananas. That will be the twenty-five sausages each that Dad and his not very slim bald mate will be having.

Now I can hear the spluttering of cans of lager being opened.

Neither of them will be able to get through the kitchen door at this rate.

Five minutes later

They must have chucked a couple of sausages out into the garden for Angus and the Pussycat Gang because there is a lot of yowling and spitting going on.

And barking.

And yelling.

Oh, here we go. Mr Next Door is on the warpath.

I looked carefully through my bedroom curtains as I didn't want the finger of shame pointing my way.

Yes, there was Mr Next Door in his combat gear (slippers and towelling robe) shouting, "Clear off!!!"

He's a fool really. Angus will think he wants to play the sausage game with the Prat Poodles.

One minute later

Ah, yes. Angus has bounded over the garden wall and he is having a sausage tug-of-war with Whitey. Mr Next Door has gone for his broom.

I'm not going to look any more as I may accidentally glimpse Mr Next Door's exposed bottom in the furore.

10:15 p.m.

Dad and the baldy-o-gram are arsing about, laughing and giggling like ninnies in the front room. Dad yelled upstairs, "Georgia, my dove, your pater and his friend are engaged in a very serious business matter. Would you get another couple of cans from the wine cellar. You may know it as the 'fridge'. Thank you so much."

I just shouted down, "Not in a million years, O Portly One."

He shouted back, "I will give you a fiver."

Huh, as if bribery is going to make me his slavey girl.

Two minutes later

When I went into the front room with the cans of lager, Dad was lying on the sofa like a great bearded whale.

Uncle Eddie winked at me as I came in.

Dad said, "So, Eddie, what is your life like, now that you are a sex symbol?" Uncle Eddie belched (charming) and said, "Well, Bob, Georgia, it has its ups and downs like most celebrity lives. For instance, last night I got mobbed by women in the chippie after the gig. Which is nice. And I got free chips and a pickled egg. But, on the other hand, when I got home I found they had bloody stolen another of my feather codpieces. Which I have to have handmade."

Oh, how vair vair disgusting. Now I have been exposed to every sort of porn in this house: mouldyporn, kittyporn, earporn and now baldyporn!!!

Speaking of kittyporn, where are Angus and Naomi? And cross-eyed Gordy?

Back in my room

It's all gone suspiciously quiet. I looked out of the window over Next Door's garden. I can't see the pussycat gang, but I can see Gordy.

Four minutes later

I am concerned that Gordy is hanging around with the wrong crowd. He is actually playing with the Prat Poodles and, I can hardly believe my eyes, he is chewing on their rubber bonio. It's not right. It's probably just an adolescent phase he is going through.

11:29 p.m.

I went down to get a drink of water and a Jammy Dodger to ward off late-night starvation. Mum came in a bit red-faced from too much *vino tinto*, or just sheer embarrassment at being her. She went into the front room where Dad and Uncle Eddie were practising some sort of dance for Uncle Eddie's act. I couldn't bear to go in and have a look, but I will just say this, the music they were using was "I'm Jake the Peg, diddle diddle diddle dum, with my extra leg" by Rolf Harris.

Mum slammed off to bed without saying goodnight.

Dad came out of the front room and said to me, "Uh-oh, women's trouble!"

Midnight

I must get away from here. I must get to see the Luuurve God. Dad owes me a fiver for being his slavey girl. So that means I have only £495 to go.

I wonder if he will believe me if I say he promised to give me £50 to get his lager?

Monday August 8th
8:30 a.m.

I am still not used to having the bed to myself. I wouldn't say I am exactly missing Libby, but I feel a space in my bed where her freezing bottom used to be. Even Angus didn't come in last night. He's probably too bloated with sausage to haul himself up the stairs.

In the Kitchen

Oh brilliant, Mutti and Vati are not speaking AGAIN. They are so childish.

Dad yelled from the bedroom, "Connie, have you seen

my undercrackers?" And Mum went on buttering her toast.

There was a long silence and then Dad said, "Er, hello... is there anybody there?"

I looked at Mum and she was chomping away on her toastie.

I said, "Mum, I would like to discuss dates with you, about my Italian holiday. Do you remember that we agreed I would go next week? Well, do you think I should travel to Rome on the Friday or the Saturday? It would be better on the Saturday because then Vati could drive me to the airport. It would be best all round, don't you think, that he hired a proper car. For safety and embarrassment reasons."

Dad yelled again from the bedroom, "Connie, stop playing the giddy goat. I'm going to be late. I cannot find any of my undercrackers."

Mum said to me, "You don't need to worry about the lift and so on."

I said, "Thanks, Mum."

She said, "You don't need to worry about a lift because you are not going anywhere."

What???

Then Dad came into the kitchen, with a towel wrapped around what he laughingly refers to as his waist. He said to

Mum, "Where are all my undercrackers?" Mum pointed to the kitchen bin.

Dad went ballisticisimus. And a half.

It didn't really seem the right moment to ask him about a lift to the airport. Or the £500 I would need for proper spendies, so I skipped back up to the safety of my room.

Fifteen minutes later

Well, it's good that the whole street knows about my dad's undercrackers and my mum's insanity. It makes for a tighter community spirit.

I do think that Dad should learn that, as our revered headmistress Slim says, "Obscene language is the language of those of a limited imagination."

Tuesday August 9th
10:00 p.m.

Jas has driven me insane today with all her Tom talk. I think she is hoping he will just forget about the going to different universities and having their own space fandango.

Well, let sleeping dogs lie is what I say.

Although it is not what Gordy says. He is worrying me.

I was calling him and tapping his food tin with a spoon earlier when Mr Next Door popped his head over the fence. He said that Gordon was sleeping in the Prat brothers' kennel.

I said, "Yeah, you'll never get him out, I'm afraid. They will have to sleep in the house."

And Mr Next Door said the weirdest thing.

"Oh, they are in there with him."

Blimey.

Wednesday August 10th

Ok, it's over a week now since I heard from Masimo, so I'm going to send a cool postcard. I've got one of a kitten covered in spaghetti being fished out of a pan with a ladle, and you can't get much cooler than that in my humble opinion. So here goes:

> Ciao, Masimo,
> It is me here. It was vair fabby and marvy to hear your voice.

Hang on, he might not know what vair means, or fabby or marvy. Blimey, it's going to take me the rest of my life to write this postcard. I'll do it tomorrow.

Thursday August 11th

I keep looking at the number I have got for Masimo. What would I say if I called him? And anyway, if he likes my eyes so much, why hasn't he got on the phone again?

Lunchtime

Even though I am plunged once more into the turbulent washing machine of luuurve, I am quite looking forward to going to Sven's dj-ing gig on Saturday.

We are having final rehearsals round at Rosie's for our backing dance routines. Honor and Sophie, the trainee Ace Gang members, are getting their big break because they are allowed to join in the rehearsal sessions. Although they won't be doing the real thing as there is not enough room on the stage and not enough ear muffs to go around. But that is showbiz for you.

We are going to do our world-renowned (well, lots of people have seen it at Stalag 14) Viking bison disco inferno dance. Also as a world premiere in honour of Sven's gig, we have come up with a dance called the Viking disco hornpipe.

It is a new departure for us as it involves costume and props. Of course, we have used props before – the horns in the Viking and bison extravaganza. And also bubble gum up the nose for the snot dance. (Incidentally, we have left out the snot dance from our programme for the night as Jools said she thought that prospective snoggees might find it a bit offputting.) So, as I say, we have used props before but we have never toyed with both costume and props.

In the Viking disco hornpipe extravaganza we will be wearing ear muffs and mittens, for the vair vair chilly Viking winter nights. And we will also be using small paddles.

At Rosie's
Evening

Jas is being annoyingly droopy.

Especially as Rosie had traipsed all the way to the fairy dressing-up shop for kiddies in town, to get the muffs. And they had special tinsel and everything. Jas wouldn't wear the ear muffs because she said it was "silly".

I said, "Jas, if we didn't do stuff just because it was silly, where would we be?"

She was still on her hufty stool and said, "What are you talking about now?"

It is vair tiring explaining things to the vair dim, but it

seems to be more or less my job in life.

"Jas, do you think that German is a silly language?"

She started fiddling with her fringe. (Incidentally, another example of 'silliness', but I didn't say.) She was obviously thinking the German thing over.

I said, "Quickly, quickly, Jas."

"Well, it's a foreign language spoken by foreign people and that can't be silly."

"Jas, they say *SPANGLEFERKEL*. The word for snogging in German-type language is *KNUTSCHEN*. WAKE UP, SMELL THE COFFEE!!!"

In the end she got her muffs and mittens on.

one hour later

The official Viking disco hornpipe dance is perfected!!!

(Just a note, costume-wise: the ear muffs are worn over the bison horns. It is imperative that the horns are not removed, otherwise it makes a laughing stock of the whole thing.) So:

The music starts with a Viking salute. Both paddles are pointed at the horns.

Then a cry of "Thor!!!" and a jump turn to the right.

Paddle, paddle, paddle, paddle to the right,

Paddle, paddle, paddle, paddle to the left.

Cry of Thor! Jump turn to the left.

Paddle, paddle, paddle, paddle to the left,

Paddle, paddle, paddle, paddle to the right.

Jump to face the front (grim Viking expression).

Quick paddle right, quick paddle left x 4.

Turn to partner.

Cross paddles with partner x 2.

Face front and high hornpipe skipping x 8 (gay Viking smiling).

Then (and this is the complicated bit) interweaving paddling! Paddle in and out of each other up and down the line, meanwhile gazing out to the left and to the right (concerned expression – this is the looking-for-land bit).

Paddle back to original position.

On-the-spot paddling till all are in line and then close eyes (for night-time rowing effect).

Right and left paddling x2 and then open eyes wide.

Shout "Land AHOYYYYY!"

Fall to knees and throw paddles in the air (behind, not in front, in case of crowd injury).

Friday August 12th
In my bedroom

> Dear Masimo,
>   Ciao. Last night we were practising our new
> Viking hornpipe dance. At first we had trouble
> with our paddles and Rosie nearly lost an eye,
> but by the high hornpipe skipping we had an...

Hang on a minute. Maybe he doesn't know what a Viking hornpipe is. Or paddles. Or skipping. Good grief, international romance is vair tiring.

Saturday August 13th
OK, if I haven't heard from the Luuurve God by the fifteenth, I will take it as a sign from Baby Jesus that I should get on the blower.

Mind you, I don't know what I would say about when I am coming over. I found £1.50 down the back of the sofa. And that would make £6.50 towards my fare except that I accidentally bought some new lip gloss (raspberry and vanilla flavour) at Boots.

Monday August 15th

10:30 a.m.

Another postcard from the Luuurve God!!! Yes, yes and three times yes! Yesittyyesyes!!!

Oh, I am so happy. He posted it ages ago, so the post in Pizza-a-gogo land must be as bad as it is here.

Two minutes later

I bet our postie has taken postie revenge for having to lug huge sacks of letters round. I bet that is what he does. I bet he doesn't deliver people's mail, he just pretends to, and he has a hut in his back garden bursting with letters and postcards.

Anyway.

The postcard has a picture of a bowl of pasta on the front and it says:

> Ciao, cara Georgia,
>   Plees come for to see me. I am having the hunger for you.
>   Masimo xxxxxxxxxxxxx

Wow wowzee wow!

That is it!! As soon as I can persuade Mum and Dad to give me spondies, I am off to see my Italian boyfriend.

Hmmm, it sounds quite groovy to say that. Not "My boyfriend that goes to Foxwood School and will probably work in a bank" but "My Italian boyfriend, who will be a world-famous pop star!"

Yessssss!

Tuesday August 16th

I tried special pleading with Mum today *vis-à-vis* money. She said, "Don't be stupid. I haven't got £500 and even if I did have, you would not be getting it to go and see some Italian bloke in Rome. Gorgey or not. You can have a tenner. Make it last."

I hate her.

Wednesday August 17th

I have gone through nearly the whole having-the-hump scale. From number one (*ignorez-vous*ing) to number six (pretendy deafnosity) and Mum hasn't even noticed.

Thursday August 18th
2:30 p.m.

Blimey, life is quite literally a boy-free zone. No sign of Dave the Laugh, no sign of Robbie. I haven't even seen the Blunder Boys around. Which is good. But weird. Even Tom has gone off to stay with some mates at uni for a few days.

Sooooo boring.

And hot.

I would do light tanning in the garden but every time I get comfy Angus comes and starts digging near me. (Not with a spade, with his paws. If he did have a spade, it wouldn't be quite so boring and annoying.)

Viking hornpipes a-gogo!!!

Saturday August 20th
Sven's Viking extravaganza gig night
6:30 p.m.

In my bedroom. I am meeting the rest of the gang at the clock tower. Jas is coming round here and we are walking up together so that she "doesn't miss Hunky". Good Lord.

We have got our ear muffs and mittens and horns in little matching vanity cases that Rosie also got from the fairy shop. She says that Sven gets a lot of his stuff from there. Blimey.

6:45 p.m.

At the back of my mind. I'm a bit worried that Robbie might turn up tonight. I know he hasn't gone off to Kiwi-a-gogo because I feel sure I would have heard it on the Radio Jas news round-up. Even if I didn't ask.

6:50 p.m.

Jas turned up at mine with her vanity case.

The vanity cases are, it has to be said, a bit on the naff side. Very pink and glittery. Jas said, "They look just like ones that fairies would use."

I gave her my "Are you mad?" look, but she didn't notice. She is too busy being a piggy-bank hogger.

However, I feel free to carry silly fairy vanity cases and to wear my horns ad hoc and willy-nilly because there is not going to be anyone at the gig that I need to impress, now that Masimo is my one and only one.

7:00 p.m.

Yippee and thrice times yippee!! I am allowed to stay at Jas's. And I don't mean my parents have allowed me to stay. Lately they don't even notice if I am in or out, they are so busy with their own 'lives'. I just said, "I am staying at Jas's tonight," and they went, "OK."

It was Jas I had to persuade to let me stay. She has been in and out of her huffmobile for the last week, but I have promised not to mess about with her owls or steal her piggy bank, so she says I can stay.

Anyway, there is no point in going home. Dad is out all the time with Uncle Eddie and his other sad portly mates, going to "gigs" or pratting around with their loonmobiles. Mum is out all the time as well because Libby is still round at Grandvati's. So, apart from the kittykats (who are also out all the time), I am practically an orphan anyway.

Buddha Lounge
8:00 p.m.
Quite cool vibe in the Buddha Lounge and rammed already. A few people I know and loads of peeps from Notre Dame School.

Jas is busy pretending that she doesn't care whether Hunky turns up or not. She thinks he might be back from his mates' tonight, but she says she has too much pridenosity to try and find out. I am not going to mention his name either,

 105

or ask about Robbie, because it will just be an excuse for her to drone on and on about the "vole years" and what larks she and Tom had by the riverside shrimping and so on. Or whatever they do. Hand snog probably, but I won't think about that now.

In the tarts' wardrobe

Ellen was in a complete ditherama and tiz wondering whether Declan would turn up. She was shaking and dithering so much that she accidentally got lipstick in her eye. That is how much she was dithering. Mabs was almost as bad about Edward.

I was tarting myself up in the mirror and said, "Oh, I am so vair vair glad that I am free to enjoy myself, unlike you lot – I shall dance, I shall let my nungas run free and wild, my nostrils can flare and obliterate my face to their heart's content. Because there is no one here tonight that I am bothered by. I am simply the girlfriend of a Luuurve God."

Mabs said, "Has he phoned since he last phoned?"

I said, "In the language of luuurve that would be called 'over-egging the pudding'."

She said, "He hasn't phoned then."

I smoothed down my internal feathers because she was slightly annoying me. Calm calm, think luuurve, think warm Italian nights and soft lips meeting in the shadow of the leaning tower of Pisa... or whatever it is they have in Rome. I said, "Actually, I am going to take the pasta by the horns and I am going to phone him and tell him that I am coming over."

Jas came out of her Tom coma. "Have your parents actually agreed that you can go? To Italy? By yourself to stay with a boy? Who is older than you?"

I tossed my hair in a tossing way like someone who has tossed their hair all over the world might do.

"*Sì.*"

All of the Ace Gang looked at me.

Jas said, "That is a big fat lie, isn't it?"

"*Sì.*"

Back on the dance floor

All right, I haven't actually got the parents to agree a date for me to go. Or give me the money or anything. But they will be too busy with the custody battle – about who doesn't get the children or the cats when they split up – to bother about me popping over to Italy for a few days.

♡ 107

That is what I feel.

I will get on the old blower tomorrow to let Masimo know I am coming, and then I will start my buttering-up-the-elderly-insane plan.

8:30 p.m.

Sven walked on to take over the decks to that song "Burn, baby, burn, disco inferno." He was wearing a fur cloak and bison horns and, joy of joys, the old lighting-up flares!! And he had his own vanity case!!! Yesssss!

The lights went crazy and he stood over his decks as we all clapped and went mental.

I said to Rosie, "You should be very, very proud. You, without the shadow of a doubt, have the maddest boyfriend in town."

She said, "I know. I can't wait to get off with him again."

8:35 p.m.

It is really alarming watching Rosie and Sven. She is dancing in front of him, sticking her bottom out at him and so on, and he is winking at her and licking his lips. I can't watch this, it's Nordyporn!!!

9:00 p.m.

Funny, there not being many people we know here. No sign of Tom or Declan or Edward or Rollo or, erm, who else – erm... oh, I know, Dave the Laugh. And his girlfriend.

I, of course, don't really mind for myself but the rest of the Ace Gang are driving me mad with all their: "Oh, I wonder why Rollo isn't here yet?"

"Oooh, I wonder where Edward is. Do you think he's with Tom and the rest and they have gone somewhere else?"

And Ellen going on and on. "Erm, it's, like, I wonder if, like, do you think that, er, Declan is, like, with Tom and the rest and they have gone somewhere else?"

I am beginning to feel a bit full of tensionosity, so I have decided to take diversionary action before I start babbling wubbish like Ellen. I said, "Let's do our dance routines now, get this party started."

I went and told Rosie, and Sven said over the microphone, "In one minute we haf the dancing girls in their horns!!!"

Rosie disentangled herself from him (which took about a million years of licking – honestly) and we dashed off to the tarts' wardrobe and got dressed in our horns. I felt so vair vair free. It must be what being a Blunder Boy feels like. No

109

matter what you do or how you are dressed, you are just not aware of being a prat.

I said, "Right, let us bond now. Group hug!!!"

We did the group hug and one quick burst of "Hoooorn!!!" And we were ready for our big moment.

Out in the club

We are gathered at the side of the little stage that Sven is on. I like to think we look attractively Nordic. With just a hint of pillaging and extreme violence about us.

For our grand finale (the Viking disco hornpipe extravaganza) we have put our paddles, ear muffs and mittens in a little pile by a speaker. All the crowd were looking at us.

Sven put on a traditional Viking song "Jingle Bells", we adjusted our horns and off we jolly well went:

Stamp, stamp to the left,

Left leg kick, kick,

Arm up,

Stab, stab to the left (that is the pillaging bit),

Stamp, stamp to the right,

Right leg kick, kick,

Arm up,

Stab, stab to the right,

Quick twirl around with both hands raised to Thor (whatever),

Raise your (pretend) drinking horn to the left,

Drinking horn to the right,

Horn to the sky,

All over body shake,

Huddly duddly,

And fall to knees with a triumphant shout of HORRRRNNNNN!!!!

It was a triumph, darling, a triumph. Even Ellen managed not to stab anyone in the eye. The crowd went berserkerama!!! Leaping and yelling, "More, more!!!"

Sven said over the mike, "OK, you groovster peeps, this time is your turn!! Let's go do the Viking bison disco inferno dance," and he put "Jingle Bells" back on and we started again.

Everyone joined in with us. The whole room did stab stab to the right, and even the huddly duddly and fall to the knees bit. It was marvy seeing everyone down on their knees yelling, "HORRRRNNN!" And people say that teenagers today do nothing for people.

I'm a star, I'm a star!!! I shouted to Jas above the noise, "I want Smarties in our dressing room. I want a limo for my mittens – I want EVERYTHING!!!"

And then it was time for the *pièce de* whatsit: the Viking disco hornpipe extravaganza. We put on our ear muffs and mittens, and picked up our paddles. Then we got into position with our backs to the crowd and when they had quietened down, we waited for our musical cue. As the dub version of *EastEnders* sounded out from the decks, we raised our paddles proudly. The music was going: "Na na na na naa naa naaaa, na na na-na naa na na na na naa naa, duff duff duff, na na na naa naa naaaa..."

We turned round to face our audience and as we did so, the doors flew open and Mark Big Gob and the Blunder Boys walked in. Oh, brilliant.

Still, what did we care? We would get our bodyguards to toss them aside like paper towels from the paper-towel dispenser in the loos. They could go down the piddly-diddly hole of life!!!

We did the dance with gusto and also vim, and everyone applauded and went crazeeee again at the end. They were yelling, "More horn, more horn. We want more horn!!!"

God, I was hot. I said to Rosie, "I can't do it again without some drink. Send one of our runners for drinks."

Rosie said, "Righty ho."

She came back a second later and said, "Who are our runners?"

And Jas said, "We haven't got any, she has just gone temporarily insane."

But she said it in a smiley way.

one minute later

We did the dance again and everyone went mad AGAIN!!! This was the life. Even though Ellen caught me a glancing blow with her paddle.

Then the Blunder Boys started shouting wubbish in their dim way.

We just ignored them and were coming down from the stage when Mark Big Gob yelled out, "Oy, you, the big tart in the middle, give us a flash of your nungas." He was shouting at Rosie.

Sven took off the record he was playing and stood up.

There was silence.

He took off his fur cape and adjusted his horns.

Oh dear God.

Sven slowly stepped down. His flares lit up and he walked towards the group of Blunder Boys. Everyone else was backing off. People were saying, "Calm down, calm down, leave it out, lads."

Well, apart from Rosie. She was behind Sven, saying, "Go on, big boy, tear their little heads off."

Two minutes later

Now Sven is big, but there were about eight of the Blunderers facing up to him. I was a bit frightened actually.

But then it was just like a Western because the doors opened again and in came Tom and Declan and Edward and Dom and Rollo and a load of their mates and, last but not least, Dave the Laugh.

Dave the Laugh looked at what was going on and then said to Mark Big Gob, "Mark, go and get your coats and handbags. You and your sisters are leaving."

Three minutes later

There was a bit of argie-bargie from the Blunder Boys.

One of them said to Dave, "Who's gonna make me leave?"

And Dave went and stood over him and said, "I am."

And the Blunder Boys said, "Oh, OK, well, I was just asking, mate."

And there was some shoving past people and spitting from the Blunder Boys as they went off to the door. Declan and Tom and Dave did a gentle bit of frogmarching Mark through the door. And there was a lot of shouting and kicking of cars once the Blunderers were safely out in the street.

Unfortunately the venue owners had called the police, and we heard the police sirens outside.

Sven said, "Now that is how to have the good Viking night."

Dave the Laugh found me. He was holding his hand as if he had hurt it. He smiled at me and said, "Are you OK, Miss Kittykat?"

I said, "Oh, Dave, thank goodness you came. What has happened to your hand?"

He said, "One of the hard lads bit me – I may never play the tambourine again."

It was luuurvely to see him. And I felt really odd that he was hurt. I wanted to stroke his hand; in fact, maybe I should. I may have healing hands.

I was just thinking about doing it when I heard a voice say, "Dave, Dave, are you all right??? Oh God, your hand!! You poor thing, let me help you."

It was Emma, dashing about like Florrie whatsit – Nightingale.

Dave looked at me and gave a sort of rueful smile. He said, "Too many trousers spoil the broth," and got up and did pretendy limping off with Emma.

His girlfriend.

Twenty minutes later

We were all turfed out. The police gave Sven a warning and asked us if we wanted to dob anyone in. I wouldn't have minded seeing the Blunder Boys behind bars, preferably in a zoo. However, as Sven had in a way started the proceedings, we just mumbled a bit about things getting out of hand. "Sorry, Officers" etc. And tried to shuffle off home.

I saw Jas and Tom talking together in the dark over by a bench. Oh Good Lord, I would be doing goosegog all the way home now if they made up.

I tried to think of something to say that would make Jas get in her huffmobile with Tom. Or perhaps I should just go and stand between them in a friendly way and not go away. Take my goosegog duties seriously.

Thirty seconds later

A policeman came by me and said, "Stop hanging about here. Clear off home now and don't cause any more trouble."

That's nice, isn't it? No words of comfort. No "Now don't you worry, young lady, the nasty boys won't be bothering you any more. Here's £5 for a cab home to see you safely on your way."

In fact, as he looked at me I sort of recognised him. Uh-oh, he was the one who had brought Angus home in a bag one night after he had eaten Next Door's hamster. Unfortunately, Angus didn't like the bag and had attacked the policeman's trousers.

Then he recognised me. "Oh, it's you. I might have known. How's your 'pet'? Hopefully gone to that big cat basket in the sky."

I said, with dignitosity at all times, "Thank you for your kind inquiry, Officer. I must go home now. Mind how you go and remember, it's a jungle out there. Be safe."

Do you see? Do you see what I did? I pretended I was a policeman to a policeman!!!

But I was walking quickly away from him as I said it and calling to Jas, "Jas, we have to go now. The nice officer of the law said so."

Jas came over smartish. She is terrified of policemen and is the bum-oley licking expert around them. She said, "Thank you so much, Officer. You do a wonderful job." Oh, pleeeeease.

Then she waved back at Tom. He blew her a kiss and she sighed. Good grief. Can't they stay split up for more than half a day? It's pathetico.

We walked on home. I said to Jas, "Did you see Dave the Laugh getting stuck in to save us?"

Jas said, "Yeah, Tom was keeping me behind him so that I wouldn't get hurt. And when one of the Blunder Boys said to him, 'Do you want some, mate?' he said, 'Oooh, fear factor ten,' and did a judo hold that we learned when we went on our survival course and just marched him to the door. It was fab."

Oh, shut up about Hunky.

I said, "When I said to Dave, 'Are you OK? Have you hurt your hand?' he said, 'I may never play the tambourine again'! He is quite literally Dave the Laugh."

Jas said, "Oh no, you've got your big red bottom AGAIN!!"
Have I?

In bed with the owl (and her mates)
1:00 a.m.

Jas has built a small barrier of owls between us, but has said that if I don't wriggle about I am allowed to sleep in her bed because it has been such a traumatic night of violence. Blimey, she should live round at my house if she thinks this has been a traumatic night of violence. My bedroom is littered with dismembered toys, and if I move in bed, I am attacked viciously by either Angus, Gordy or Libby. Or all three of them.

Jas said, "Tom still thinks we should go to different unis or see the world or something. He said we might never know if we have done the right thing otherwise. But it doesn't mean he doesn't love me."

I said, "Well, what do you think?"

She mused (that is, flicked her fringe and cuddled Snowy Owl). "Well, I like fun as much as the next person."

I said, "Can I just stop you there, Jas. You have to be realistic if we are going to get anywhere. You do not like fun as much as the next person. Your idea of fun and the next person's idea of fun are vair vair different."

"Well, all right, what I mean is, maybe Tom is right that we are too young to decide everything now. Maybe I could do things by myself and that would be good."

I sat up. "That is the ticket, pally. I mean, there are many advantages to not having a boyfriend, you know. You wouldn't have to pretend to be interested in wombat droppings and varieties of frogspawn."

She looked puzzled. "I'm not pretending."

"Er, right, well..."

God, it was hopeless. Everything I thought of, Jas had an answer for. She doesn't want to let her red bottom run free and wild. She doesn't mind the vole-dropping stuff and looking interested. She IS interested. She doesn't want to flop around in her jimmyjams if she wants to because she already can, because Tom, Hunky the Wonderdog, likes her just the way she is, whatever she looks like.

In a nutshell, Tom is her one and only one and that is the end of the matter. I wish I were her.

Well, of course I don't wish I were her. That would be ridiculous. I'd have to chop my own head off for a start, because I'd be annoying myself so much.

Sunday August 21st

I have got post-gig comedown, I think. Everything was tickety-boo when we were doing the dancing and it was a laugh. And even the fight was sort of exciting. But then seeing Dave the Laugh go off with Emma, and Jas talking about being with Hunky, it's sort of made me a bit full of glumnosity.

And I haven't spoken to the Luuurve God for ages; anything could be happening.

Boo and also poo.

It's all gloomy in the house: even though it is sunny outside it is raining inside. Well, not really, but you know what I mean. Mum has gone off with Libby, I think trying to placate Josh's mum. I'd like to think it's because she cares, but really I think it's because Grandvati has gone off for a camping trip with Maisie. She has probably knitted the tent. Who knows where Vati is; he is never in these days.

I didn't think the day would ever come when I said this, but I wish they would get back to 'normal'. I would even try not to be sick if they touched each other.

What if they split up? They would make me do that choosing thing. The judge would say that I could decide who I lived with.

It is so clearly not going to be Dad. I may warn him that he is dicing with never seeing me again by his brutal lack of care for me. He will not give me the least thing. I tried to ask him for a couple of hundred squids towards my trip to Rome yesterday, and he laughed.

Two minutes later
I wonder if he will laugh quite so much when all he has to remember me by are the press cuttings of me on world tours etc. Doing backing dancing for the Stiff Dylans in exotic locations. And when I do interviews in showbiz mags, and they ask me about my father, I will say, "I would have liked to have been close, but once the family split up and my work took me all over the world, I sort of outgrew him."

I won't add "like he outgrew his trousers" because that would put me in a bad light pop culture-wise.

Five minutes later
Hey, maybe I could say that if he will give me £500 to go to

Pizza-a-gogo, I will consider seeing him three or four times a year for an afternoon.

Excellent plan!!!

Ten minutes later

Phone rang. At last. I bet this will be my Pizza-a-gogo Luuurve God-type boyfriend on the blower from Roma *bella*. I have got an Italian book for idiots, so I must look through it. Mind you, if it is anything like our French or German textbooks it will be rubbish. They are always to do with losing your bike. They are not based on real life; there is nothing about how to snog in different languages. Absoluto stupido and uselessio.

And also too late-io.

I picked up the phone and said, "*Ciao!*"

"Oh, erm, *ciao* or something – er – I, well, it's me or something. I don't know if—"

"Hello, Ellen."

"Georgia... Could I – I mean, are you in?"

"No, I'm sorry, I'm not."

"Oh, well, will you be in later or something?"

"ELLEN, I am answering the phone. How can I not be in???"

Half an hour of ditherosity later

Miracle of miracles, Declan has actually asked her on a date. They're meeting by the clock tower tomorrow evening, so she has come to the Luuurve Goddess (*moi*) for advice.

It passes the time helping others.

I said, "Ellen, here in a nutshell are my main top tips. Don't drink or eat anything, not even a cappuccino, unless you know for sure your date is an admirer of the foam moustache. If he is – dump him. Secondly and vair vair importantly, do not say what is in your brain. And, above all, remember to dance and be jolly. Although be careful about where you do spontaneous dancing. If you do it in a supermarket, he will just think you are weird."

4:00 p.m.

Right, this is it. I can't stand waiting any more. I am going to quite literally take the Luuurve God by the horns and ring him up.

I've been going through my Italian book for the very very dim. (It's not actually called that, but it should be. It has got the crappest drawings known to humanity. I think it must be the same person who did the illustrations for our German textbook about the Koch family. Under the section "Fun and Games" it has got a drawing of some madman with sticky-up hair and big googly eyes juggling balls. That cannot be right in anyone's language.)

Anyway, I have worked out what to say from the section called "Talking on the Phone".

4:30 p.m.
I think I have got the code right and everything.

Rang the number. Ring ring. Funny ring they have in Pizza-a-gogo land.

The phone was picked up and I said, "*Ciao.*"

A man's voice said, a bit hesitantly, "*Ciao.*"

I wondered if it was Masimo's dad. What is the word for "dad" in Italian? I hadn't looked it up. It couldn't be "daddio", could it?

I thought I would try. "Er, *buon giorno,* daddio, *je suis* – erm, *non non* – *sono* Georgia."

"Georgia."

"*Sì.*"

Masimo's dad said, "Ah, *sì.*" Then there was a bit of a silence.

♡ 125

Oh, buggeration. How do I say I want to speak to Masimo? I said, "Io wantio – *un momento, per favore.*"

I scrabbled through the book. Oh here we are, a lovely big ear drawing to show me that it is the on-the-phone section. "I want to speak to..." I read it out slowly and loudly: "*POSSO PAHR-LAH-REH A MASIMO?*"

There was a silence and then a Yorkshire voice said, "Po what, love? You've lost me."

It turned out that I was actually speaking to a Yorkshire bloke on holiday in Rome.

I said, "Oh, I'm sorry, but you said *ciao* and I thought you were Italian."

The Yorkshire dad said, "No, I'm from Leeds, but I do like spaghetti."

Two minutes later

Anyway, he was having a lovely time, although you couldn't get a decent pickled egg in Roma apparently, but he wasn't letting that spoil his fun.

Blimey, it was like a Yorkshire version of Uncle Eddie. He was rambling on for ages like I knew him.

Ten minutes later

In the end I got off the phone. I must have got the number wrong. Or misdialled it. I could try again. No, I couldn't take the risk of getting hold of "Just call me Fat Bob" again.

Big furry paw of fate

Tuesday August 23rd
In the kitchen
5:30 p.m.

My darling sis is back at Chaos Headquarters (that is our house). Mum said, "I've managed to get Libby off with a warning. She can go back to nursery later this week, but I have to promise that she won't be allowed to play with sharp implements. So don't let her have any of your knives and so on."

"Mum, I haven't got any knives. It was you that let her have the scissors to cut Pantalitzer doll's hair. Has Josh got the word BUM off his forehead yet?"

Mum said, "Blimey, that was a fuss and a half, wasn't it? It was only indelible ink, not poison."

I said, "Mum, some parents actually, like, DO parenting. They act like grown-ups; they protect their young."

Mum was too busy flicking through *Teen Vogue* to listen.

6:00 p.m.

Libby is preparing a cat picnic on the lawn. Some crushed-up biscuits on a plate and three dishes of milk. I can see Angus, Naomi and Gordy skulking off to hide. They have been made to go to her cat picnics before. And once you have had your head shoved violently into a saucer of milk and a spoonful of Jammy Dodger rammed down your throat, you don't accept another invitation easily.

Time to start buttering up the mutti.

I said, "Mum, if I stayed with you and not Dad, well he would pay like maintenance and child support and so on. And I could use a bit of it, say like £500, because it would be mine really, wouldn't it? It's like me that is being supported, isn't it?"

Mum went, "Hmmm, but I would need a lot of help round the house."

♥ 129

I said, "Yep, yep, I could do that. It would be like sort of earning my own money and I could pay my own way to Pizza-a-gogo land and then it would be all right, wouldn't it? Because actually it wouldn't really be costing you anything because I would be being paid out of my own money really. And you want me to be happy and have a boyfriend and so on; even Ellen has got a boyfriend now. And when you leave Dad you might get one. You never know. Never say never."

Mum said, "Georgia, are you saying that you would be prepared to do the ironing and help around the house and be pleasant?"

I said, "Oh, *mais oui*, yes!!"

"OK, well, start on that big pile of Libby's stuff in the washing basket."

Lalalalalala. It's the ironing life for me. Quickly followed by a snogtastic adventure in Luuurve God Heaven.

Half an hour later

How boring is housework? I tell you this for free, I will not be doing any more of it when this is over. I said to Mum, "I think I have got ironer's elbow. It won't go from side to side any more, it will only go up and down. I hope it hasn't ruined my backing dancing career."

7:15 p.m.
I am a domestic husk.

I said to Mum, "I think I will go on Saturday as I suggested."

She said, "Yeah, good idea."

I said, "I will ask Dad if he can drop me off at the airport."

"He's away that weekend, he and Uncle Eddie are going away fishing or prancing around in the clownmobile. He says it will give him time to sort his mind out."

I said, "So can you take me then?"

"Take you where?"

"To the airport."

"Why are you so interested in watching planes all of a sudden?"

"I'm not interested in watching them. I am only interested in getting on one to go to Pizza-a-gogo."

"Well, that is not going to happen, is it."

And that was that.

She never intended to let me go, she just wanted me to do

the ironing. That is the sort of criminal behaviour I have to put up with. I know you read all sorts of miserable stories about kids being holed up in cellars by their mean parents and called "Snot Boy" all the time, but I think my story is just as cruel.

As I slammed out I said to Mum, "Mum, I quite literally hate you."

At Rosie's in her bedroom
8:00 p.m.

Rosie's parents are out again. It's bliss at her house. I think she only sees them about twice a year. I told her what happened. She said, "That is crapola, little matey. When you are all stressed out and having a nervy spaz you have to look after your health – have a Jammy Dodger and some cheesy wotsits."

As we crunched through a couple of packets I said, "I am just going to sneak off anyway, creep out at night with the money I will get from my guilty dad and hitchhike to the airport. Or maybe get one of the lads to take me. Do you think Dom might do it?"

Rosie was really into it now. "Brilliant plan. Just say, devil take the hindmost and *ciao*, Roma!!!"

9:00 p.m.

I was going to call Dom about taking me to the airport, but I sort of chickened out. If I could, I would ask Dave the Laugh because he would understand. Or maybe not. Maybe asking my matey-type matey person to take me to catch a plane to see a Luuurve God is not megacool.

Anyway, he would only go on about my lesbian affair with Masimo.

Still at Rosie's
9:20 p.m.

Making a list of what to take with me clothes and make-up-wise. It will be hot, so I will have to take most of my summerwear, bikinis and flip-flops.

I said, "Do you think I should take a book to read on the beach for those quiet moments?"

Rosie looked at me. "What quiet moments?"

10:00 p.m.

Oh, I feel quite pepped up now. In fact, I think I will start packing when I get in.

As I was leaving Rosie's I said, "Thank you, tip-top pally."

 133

She said, "*De rigueur.* Hey, and don't forget your passport, chum."

I laughed.

On the way home
Fifteen minutes later

Hmmm, where is my passport?

An hour later

I'll tell you where my passport is. At Dad's bloody office, that's where.

Why? What sort of person takes official documents to work with them?

My dad, that is what sort of person.

I said to him, "Why would anyone do that?"

He said, "They're all there. I know you, you would lose yours or put make-up on it or Angus would eat it. This way I know where it is."

I said, "Well, now I know where it is as well, so why don't you go and get me MY passport. Which is issued to me in MY name. By her Maj the Queen. Because it is MY passport. Do you see? Not yours. And while you are in the safe, you may as well get me the £500 child support you promised me."

He said no.

I said to Dad as I stormed off to bed, "Dad, I quite literally hate you."

Ten minutes later

So this is my life:

I am best friends with some Yorkshire bloke called Fat Bob.

I will have to explain to my marvy and groovy new pop idol Luuurve God boyfriend that I am not allowed my own passport.

And I have got £1.50 to get to Pizza-a-gogo land.

What could be worse?

Midnight

Libby put an egg under my pillow to "get a baby chicken".

It has gone all over my pyjamas.

Wednesday August 24th

8:00 a.m.

I am the prisoner of my utterly useless and mean parents. Just because they have a crap life they are determined to make mine crap as well. I would have said that to them if I were speaking to them. Or they were speaking to each other.

In my bedroom

Dad came knocking on my door.

I said, "The door is locked."

Dad pushed open the door and said, "You haven't got a lock on your door."

I said, "You might not see the lock but the lock is there, otherwise I wouldn't be."

But he's not interested in me. He said, "Look, I am going away for a few days and—"

I said, "What is it like to be able to walk around on the planet wherever you like?"

He said, "You're not still going on about visiting this Italian Stallion lad, are you? He'll be back in a week or two anyway."

"Dad, I might not be alive in a week or two – things happen. If I were a mayfly, I would be dead in about half an hour and that would have been my whole life."

He just looked all grumpy, like a big leatherette grumpy fool. What was he wearing? A leather jacket.

I said, "You're not thinking of going out in that jacket, are you?"

136

He said, "Look, don't start. I've just come to say goodbye and to say that, well... you know that Mum and I have been, you know, not hitting it off."

"She threw your undercrackers away."

"I know she bloody did. Most of them were covered in cat litter when I fished them out."

Oh really, do I have to listen to this sort of thing? I will quite literally spend most of my superstar money on psychiatric fees. He still hadn't finished though.

"Don't worry too much, we'll sort it out, and if, well, if things don't get any better, sometimes people have to..."

Oh no, I think he might be going to get emotional. If he starts crying, I may well be sick. But then he did something much, much worse; he came over and kissed the top of my head.

How annoying. And odd.

One hour later

As Mum went off to "work" she said, "You look a bit peaky."

I said, "It's probably a symptom of my crap life. Which is your fault."

She just ignored me.

I know what she is up to though. She isn't bothered about

137

me having rickets or something, she just fancies a trip to Dr Clooney's. That will be the next thing. She'll start peering at me and saying stuff about my knees being a bit knobbly or that I don't blink enough or something and then suggest a quick visit to the surgery. She will have to drag me there.

10:40 a.m.

The post arrived. I may as well check if there is anything for me.

One minute later

Oh joy unbounded, there is a postcard from the Luuurve God!! It has a picture of a donkey drinking a bottle of wine on the front. Is that what goes on in Rome? You never know with not-English people.

Shut up, brain, and read the postcard from the beluuurved.

> *Ciao, bella.*
> *I am mis you like crazy. I am not for long to wait to see you. Todaya we go to the mountains. I have song in my heart for you.*
> *Masimo xxxxxxx*

Aaaaaahhhh. He has a song in his heart for me. I hope it is not "Shut uppa you face, whatsa matta you". Or, as it is in the beautiful language of Pizza-a-gogo land, "Shut uppa you face, whatsa matta you".

Oh, I sooo want to see him.

I wonder if I had a whip-round of the Ace Gang I could get the money. I bet Jas has got hundreds stashed in her piggy bank. But then what about my passport? Maybe I could make a forgery?

I HATE my parents.

Evening
To celebrate our last days of freedom before we get sent back to Stalag 14, we have decided to have a spontaneous girls' night in. We are all staying round at Jools's place because she has her own sort of upstairs area with her own TV and bathroom.

Now that is what I call proper parenting. Getting a house big enough so that you don't actually have to have anything to do with your parents. No growing girl should ever run the risk of seeing either her mutti or vati in undercrackers.

11:00 p.m.
I've perked up a bit.

Rosie, Jools, Mabs and me are in one huge bed and Jas, Ellen, Honor and Sophie are in the other one.

Jas amazed me by saying, "Actually, it's quite nice being single for a bit, isn't it? You can really let yourself go mad and wild. I mean, this is the first time I've worn my Snoopy T-shirt for ages."

I said, "Blimey, Jas, calm down."

Rosie said, "What we all have to remember is that yes, boys and snogging are good, but luuurve with a boy may be temporary and Miss Selfridge and Boots are yours for life."

Vair vair wise words. Then we got down to serious business.

Mabs said, "Well, I dunno really, what do you think of this? I saw Edward in the street, across the road with his mates, and he did that phone thing... you know when you pretend you have got a phone in your hand and you do a dial thing. Meaning, you know, bell me."

We all looked at her.

I said, "So have you?"

She said, "No, because I didn't know if he meant, like, I'm going to bell you or you should bell me. I'm sort of all..."

I said, "Belled up?"

And she nodded.

Blimey.

This was worse than s'laters.

We've decided that Mabs can't take the risk of an ad-hoc bell-you fandango and therefore the only thing to do is to accidentally bump into him and see what happens.

Jools said, "I know that they play five-a-side in the park on Thursday arvies, so we could accidentally on purpose be there. The last time I saw Rollo he said the same to me. He said, 'Give us a bell.' But then I did and he seemed sort of busy. He was on his way out to practice and he said, 'Give us a bell later.' But I didn't because that was like a double fandango: give us a bell and also s'later. Nightmare scenario."

Hmmmmm.

Then Ellen told us about going out with Declan.

I said, "Please don't tell me you went to a penknife shop for the evening."

Ellen said, "No, we, well – erm... he and I—"

I said, "I know you feel sort of sensitive about this and, you

 141

know, shy and a bit self-conscious, but you are among your own kind now; you are with the Ace Gang – your best pallies, your bestiest most kindiest maties. So let me put it this way – WHAT NUMBER DID YOU GET UP TO ON THE SNOGGING SCALE AND ARE YOU GOING TO SEE HIM AGAIN???"

Forty years later

So, just to save precious hours, I will sum up Ellen's evening with Declan. After a lot of chatting and Coke drinking (good choice drink-wise *vis-à-vis* foam moustache etc.), Declan had said goodnight and they had done one, two, three and a bit of four. Hurrah, thank the Lord!!!

On the down side, as she went into her house Declan had said, "We must do this again sometime." And gone off.

We decided that "sometime" is in fact s'laters in disguise.

I told them my mum's theory about boys being gazelles in trousers that must be enticed out of the woods (i.e. away from their stupid mates). We decided that the best thing was to be alert for sightings of the gazelles (playing footie etc.) and to be attractively semi-available.

Jas then got all misty-eyed about first meeting Tom. She said to me, "Do you remember when I first saw Tom and he was so hunky, working in the shop? And we had a plan to make him notice me. And I went into the shop to buy some onions and then you came in and made out like I was the most popular girl in the school sort of thing. And the rest is history."

She looked a bit sad and said, "Quite literally, the rest might be history."

To cheer her up, and also to stop her moaning on about the vole years, I suggested we get down to talking about serious world matters. Like the beret question for winter term. Could we improve on last year's lunchpack theme?

Sophie said, "My very favouritist was 'glove animal'. Couldn't he come back for a reprise this term?"

Midnight

We were comparing notes snogging-scale-wise and also saying what number we thought people had got to.

Jools said, "Do you think Miss Wilson has ever snogged anyone? If so, what number do you think she has got up to?" Erlack.

I said, "No man alive could get through all that corduroy."

Rosie said, "Oh, I don't know, she has a certain charm. I think I may be on the turn actually, because I thought she looked quite fit when I saw her in the nuddy-pants with her soap on a rope."

We all looked at her. Sometimes even I am surprised by how mad and weird she is.

I said, "Jools, swap places with me. I am not sleeping next to Lezzie Mees." And then Rosie started puckering up at me. I stood up in bed and started kicking her off and she grabbed my ankles and pulled me over.

Mabs yelled, "Girl fight, girl fight!" and we started a massive pillow fight. At which point the door opened and Jools's mum came in. Oh dear.

She looked very serious. Here we go with the "We give you girls a bit of freedom and you just take advantage, when I was a girl we didn't even have pillows, we slept in a drawer and—"

But she just said, "Georgia, your mum is on the phone for you. You can take it on the extension up here if you like, dear."

I wondered why she was looking at me so funny? Maybe Mum was drunk on *vino tinto* and having an Abba evening with her friends and had decided to start a new life with a fireman that she met at aquarobics. Well, I tell you this for free, I am not going to live with her and Des or whatever he is called.

Mum was actually crying when I picked up the phone. Oh

brilliant, she had already been dumped by Des and I would have to listen to her rambling on about it for the rest of my life.

She said, "Oh, darling, I am so, so sorry." Then she started crying again.

I said, "Er, Mum, I will not be moving in with you and Des."

She didn't even bother to reply; she was just gulping and crying. Actually, I was a bit worried about her because she did sound very upset. Oh blimey.

She went on, "Mr Across the Road came over – and oh, it was so – when I opened the door, I thought, I thought he was carrying a baby – all wrapped up in a blanket... and then, oh love, and... and, oh, one of his paws fell out of the, out of the blanket and it just... hung there... all limp."

And she started weeping and weeping. I couldn't understand what she meant.

I said, "What do you mean? Whose paw?"

And she said, "Oh, darling, it's Angus."

I couldn't speak and my brain wouldn't work. I could hear Mum sobbing and talking but she sounded like a little toyperson on the end of the phone.

"Mr Across the Road found him at the bottom... of our street... by the side of the road – you know how much he liked

 145

cars... he, he thought they were big mice on wheels, didn't he – and he must have been – and he was just lying there."

Then tears started coming out of my eyes, all by themselves, just pouring out of my eyes and plopping on my pyjamas. My mouth was dry, and I felt like I was choking on something.

Mum was still talking. "Georgia, love, please talk to me. Please say something, please."

I don't know how long I stood there with the tears falling, but then I felt a big pain in my heart like someone had kicked it and then stuck a knife in it. And I think a noise came out of me – you know, like when people are in pain and they make like a deep groan. It didn't feel like my voice, just like someone in pain very far away.

I think it must have been real because the next thing I knew Jas had her hand on my shoulder. She said, "What's happened, Gee? What's the matter?"

I couldn't say. I could only cry and shake. Jas took the phone out of my hand.

"Hello? It's Jas. What has happened? Oh no. Oh no."

As she was speaking Jas had her arm around me. "Yes, yes, I'm here. I'll look after her. I'll come with her in a taxi. Yes, yes, I'll look after her. We are all here; we'll take care of her."

By now the Ace Gang had come out into the hall and when they saw me, they all came and hugged me. I just wanted to be unconscious, I think. I wanted to tear my head off so it wouldn't have anything in it.

I can't really remember what happened, but I know I was shaking so much that Jools's mum wrapped me in a big blanket, and then the taxi arrived. I cried and cried into Jas's shoulder and she made those noises that people do – not really words, just like "there, there – sshhhh" – like you do when little children have nightmares. She was rocking me.

When we got to our house all the lights were on in the front room. I could see Mum looking out of the window as we pulled into the driveway.

When I tried to get out of the cab I couldn't make my legs work and the cab driver got out of his seat and came and picked me up. He said, "Don't worry, love, I've got you."

He carried me into the house and when he put me down, Mum and Jas got hold of an arm each to make me safe. As he went the cab driver said, "Look after her, there's no charge. God bless."

My voice was all croaky when I tried to speak. I said, "Where... is he?"

And Mum said, "I put him on the sofa."

It was really weird going into the front room. It was like a gale-force wind was blowing; I was sure it was real. I could hear it whooshing against the door, trying to keep me out. I felt like I was walking into the wind trying to get to Angus.

He was on the sofa wrapped up in the blanket. His eyes were all closed and his mouth half open. There was a big deep red gash on his head. I went over to him and looked down and my tears splashed on to his face. How could I live without my furry pal? He wasn't supposed to leave me. In that moment I would rather it was me lying there.

I sat down beside him and put my finger on his nose and stroked it. It was the first time I had ever been able to do that. He would have attacked my hand when he – when he – and I started wailing again, just saying, "Oh, Angus, Angus, I love you, I love you more than anything."

And then a little noise came out of him. Like a little growl. I yelled, "Mum, Mum, he's alive!!! He's moving!!! He's alive!!!"

Mum came over and put her arms around me. "I know he's still breathing, love, but when I phoned the vet I told him what had happened and what he looked like. The vet said he would have internal injuries and that really the best, the kindest thing, would be to put him to sleep. He's coming over now and going to take him to the surgery and—"

I leaped up. "He is NOT going to be put to sleep. If anyone tries to do that, I will KILL them. I mean it, Mum. It is NOT going to happen. No, you can't let him. I won't let him."

The doorbell rang.

Thirty seconds later

I must have looked like I was going to kill the vet. He looked at me and then said, "Let me have a look at the poor fellow."

He gently felt all over Angus and lifted up his legs. They just flopped back. Angus didn't make any more noises.

The vet sighed. He said, "I'm afraid there will be a lot of internal injury. I think the kindest thing all round would be—"

I just said, "No."

The vet looked at me. He shook his head.

I said, "Please try. I love him." And the tears started plopping out of my eyes again.

I stroked Angus's face and he did a bit of a growl again.

I said to the vet, "You see?"

After a minute or two the vet said, "All right, I'll try,

but I'm being honest with you, cats don't often survive this sort of thing."

He packed Angus in blankets and said he would give him X-rays and drips and anything he could at the surgery.

I said, "Thank you."

I didn't mean to but I gave him a hug.

And he's got a beard.

Vet's surgery

Angus has bandages everywhere, even on his tail. He has not made any noise since the little one when I stroked his face. He is on a drip and his tongue is lolling out.

But I am not annoyed about his tongue lolling out. I can't imagine ever being annoyed with him again about anything. If he lives, he can have anything he wants.

I said to Jas, who was still with me, "When I get home I am going to pray for Angus to Baby Jesus, and if he will let Angus live I will try to be a really good person." And I included Jas's fringe flicking in that. And my dad's leather trousers. That is how serious it all was.

Angus was going to stay in the surgery overnight and the vet said I could come the next day as soon as they opened.

He looked tired and a bit sad. And now I noticed it he also looked very beardy. No, no, I don't want the tired and sad beardy vet. I want the handsome, thrusting ER vet who says, "I've done it, he's going to pull through. Have a nice day."

Dr Beardy said, "I want you to know that I love animals very much, and I know what he means to you, but it doesn't look good. If I keep him alive, he will probably die in a few hours from something I can't fix."

I just said, "He is not going to die. That is a fact."

Jas said she'd come and stay with me at my house but I said no. I wanted to do some heavy praying. She gave me a little kiss on the cheek when she left. I know it was dark and a lezzie-free zone, but it was still nice of her.

Thursday August 25th

Dawn

I don't think I slept. I just nodded off now and again and then woke up, and for a few moments life felt normal and then I remembered. Even Gordy, not world-renowned for his caring, sympathetic nature, cuddled up next to me and didn't attack me once even when I moved my foot.

Five minutes later

Gordy came and sat on my chest and looked at me with his yellow eyes. Well, one of his yellow eyes; the other one was glancing out of the window. He was looking at me unblinking. Then he let out one of those strange croaky noises that makes him sound like he is a hundred-a-day smoking cat. And he leaped down from my bed.

I think he knows something. I think he knows about Angus and he is on my side.

Even if he is a homosexualist half-cat half-dog, it doesn't matter. Love is all you need.

Ten minutes later

Looking out of the window, Gordy is playing chase the bonio with the Prat brothers.

That is not right in anyone's book.

To think of his father lying in a vet's surgery while his son scampers around with ridiculous poodles. He has no pridenosity.

Five minutes later

I remembered my vow to Baby Jesus – about being a jolly good egg about everything. Even very annoying things.

Deep breath and – look, look at Gordy playing happily with other creatures made by God.

All right, curly, annoying yappy creatures, but God's creatures nevertheless.

I mean, not many people like maggots, do they? But that is not the point. Mr and Mrs Maggot love them. Probably. And that is what counts.

Oh shut up, brain. Just love everything and get on with it.

7:30 a.m.

Please let him be alive. Please.

I started to get myself some Coco Pops, but I couldn't eat them. Mum got up and her eyes were all swollen. I went into the bathroom and looked in the mirror. Blimey, I had no eyes. They had disappeared in the night. I was now just a nose with two eyebrows. And the places where my eyes had been ached and ached. In fact, everything ached.

Mum said, "I think I am going to ask Grandad now he's back if Bibbs can stay there for a couple of days just until this is all over – I mean, you know..."

I said, "Just until Angus comes home for convalescence you mean?"

Mum looked at me. "Georgia... you know what the vet said."

I shouted, "What does he know? His beard is so bushy, he probably can't even see what animal he's treating unless it says 'Who's a pretty boy then?' Or starts barking or neighing."

Mum said, "Calm down. He's doing his best."

I said, "He'd better be."

one minute later

Hello, God and Baby Jesus, erm, I might have given the wrong impression about Dr Beardy the vet in that I implied he was a beardy fool. But I meant it in a lighthearted and gay way.

one minute later

When I say "gay" I don't mean gay as in an "OOOOhhhh, do you like my big beard?" sort of way. I mean that I was merely being cheerful.

one minute later

Dear G and BJ, I am signing off communication-wise as

I have to go to the piddly-diddly department.

Surgery
9:00 a.m.

I had awful collywobbles tum trouble as we waited. The nurse took us down to the cat cages bit. It was so sad in there. Doped-up kittykats with drips and bandages and charts. We went over to Angus's cage and he was just lying there. He didn't look like he had moved since last night. But the little machine was going *click click*, so he was breathing.

Dr Beardy came in and said, "No change, I'm afraid. I think you had better try and prepare yourselves for him to go. All his internal organs are so swollen up from the impact, I can't tell what damage has been done, but there is sure to be some bleeding, and then—"

At home
11:00 a.m.

Mum has gone to work. She said she would call in sick and stay with me, but I know she will get into trouble. And anyway, she will get bored and start telling me stuff about her and Dad and her inner dolphin. Or how she wants to fulfil her creativity by becoming a belly dancer at firemen's balls.

So, all in all, it's better to be by myself.

Five minutes later
I am so restless, I don't know what to do.

Ten minutes later
Jas rang. The Ace Gang are going for a ramble. Just a casual ramble to the park. But actually I know it is because they hope that the lads will be playing footie and that they can accidentally bump into them to solve the s'later and "sometime" fandango.

Jas was being very nice actually, although she was chewing. I didn't say anything because of my vow of nicenosity. She said, "Come with us. It will take your mind off things. You can get a nice tan while you are miserable. That would be good for when Masimo comes back."

She is being sweet to me, and she was a big pally cuddling me and looking after me when I heard about Angus. And I know she is miz about Tom, so I said I would go.

In the park

Phew, it's bloody boiling. We are all lolling under a tree. We are doing leg tanning again by having our legs in the sun and the rest of us underneath the shade of the tree. Well, apart from Rosie, who has her own method of tanning. She makes Sven stand over her head with his jacket held out to make a nice cool shadow. He is burbling on in a Sven way.

It's quite soothing listening to him talk. As Jools said, "It takes your mind off things because it sounds like it should make sense, but it doesn't."

He was saying, "*Ja* and when I take you my bride, Rosie, to my people, they will laugh and sing and kill the herring and make the hats with the herrings."

This can't possibly be true.

I said to Rosie, "Is Sven saying that his mum and dad will make you a herring hat?"

She said, "Yes, exciting, isn't it?"

Then we heard Rollo yelling from across the park. "Oy, Sven, fancy a game of footie, mate?" And Sven went off.

I sat up and I could see Rollo, Tom, Declan, Edward and Dom having a kick about.

Ellen, Jas, Jools and Mabs immediately lost their marbles.

They were trying to hide behind the tree trunk to put more make-up on.

Jools was saying, "Oh my God, do you think Rollo saw my legs? They are so pale. They didn't look so bad in the house but now I'm practically blinded by them."

Mabs said, "Do you think this is a lurking lurker on my chin or a dimple?"

Even Jas had gone into mad fringe-flicking mode. And Ellen practically dithered her own head off.

I just looked at them. How very superficial it all seemed. I don't think I could ever really care what I looked like again. I might even stop shaving my legs.

In fact, that is what I could say to Baby Jesus if he lets Angus be all right. As a mark of solidarity with my injured furry friend, I will let my own body hair run free and wild. It can shoot happily out of the back of my knees or grow so long in my underarms that I can make it into small plaits.

I won't care.

Thirty seconds later

I don't think even a wrathful god would demand that I went as far as the one mono eyebrow though.

Jools was looking over at the lads kicking a ball about. "Do you think they will come over?"

Mabs said, "Do you think we should amble over there to be a bit nearer, or is that like breaking the rubber-band rule?"

Ellen said, "Er what, I mean, what is like, the rubber band rule, or something?"

Mabs said, "You know, what Georgia told us from that *How to Make Any Twit Fall in Love with You* book, where you have to display glaciosity and let them come pinging back like a rubber band."

We were saved from thinking about a plan by what happened next.

Robbie arrived on his scooter and on the back was Wet Lindsay.

Bloody Nora. Everyone looked at me.

What was she doing on the back of his scooter? He hadn't even had a scooter the last time I saw him. Perhaps he was trying to be like the Luuurve God. How weird.

Not as weird as having Wet Lindsay clinging round your waist though.

Then, as they took their helmets off, Dave the Laugh arrived through the trees holding hands with Emma.

 159

The Ace Gang looked at me again.

Rosie said, "Crikey."

Five minutes later

Everyone else wants to go over and watch the lads play and find out what's going on.

If I don't go, it will look like I really care about what Robbie and Ms Slimy-no-forehead-knobbly-arse are doing together. Or it might seem that I am avoiding seeing Dave the Laugh and Emma. I am quite literally surrounded by *ordure* and poo.

After a squillion years of tarting up (not me, the others. I just put on some lippy... well, and a bit of mascara and eyeliner... and face bronzer... but I only did it to be brave, not for vanitosity like the rest), we all walked over to the lads. I was right at the back. I must remember I am the girlfriend of a Luuurve God. As we got to the sidelines the lads went on playing but they were whistling and calling out stuff to us.

Rollo said, "Back off, girls, this is a man's game."

And Declan said, "Look at this for ball skills... whey hey!!!" and he headed the ball right into the goal (two coats and a can of Fanta). Then he bent down, pretended to sniff the grass and banged his bottom with his hands. And all the other boys did the same. I will say it again, because I never tire of saying it, boys are truly, truly weird.

Dave and Robbie were getting their footie boots on. Wet Lindsay looked daggers at me when she saw me. She was sitting on the back of the scooter wearing some ridiculous short skirt. How very naff to wear that on the back of a scooter. I would never do that. Well, I had done it, but I would never do it like her.

I looked away from her. I must say something loudly about Masimo in a minute. I was saved the trouble by Dom yelling out as he passed by dribbling the ball. "I got a bell from Mas and he said you were off to Pizza-a-gogo land – *hasta la vista*, baby."

And then he was viciously tackled from behind by Sven and there was a bit of an argie-bargie.

Everyone's attention was on the rumpus and I sort of sensed someone behind me. It was Robbie. I looked round at him. He looked at me very seriously. He was about to say something when Wet Lindsay called out, "Robbie, hon, could you fetch me a Coke before you go on?"

He hesitated and then turned round and said, "Sure, babe," and went off to the sweet stall. How amazingly naff and weird.

Lindsay got off the scooter and came over to me. The rest of the gang were crowded round the arguing lads and so she got me on my own. She stood right next to me and said, "If you mess this up for me, Nicolson, your life will not be worth living at school. I am head girl this year and believe me, if there is any way I can make your life difficult, I will. He's mine this time; he's sick of losers. Ta taa." And she slimed off.

Oh marvellous! How I am looking forward to Stalag 14. Not.

Then I remembered Angus and I thought, if he doesn't live, I'm not even going to go back to school. I'll get a job, or do voluntary service in a kittykat home abroad or something. I wonder how he is?

All by himself in the vet's. Maybe he's all lonely and frightened. Or in pain. Or...

I had to see him so I decided I would go to the surgery and find out what was happening. I wouldn't bother telling the others; they would understand, and besides, they were too busy tarting around in front of the lads.

I started walking off towards the gates. I had to pass quite near Dave and Emma. Dave was just about to join in the game. I must try for a naturalosity-at-all-times sort of attitude.

As I went by I said cheerily, "Hi, Emma, Dave, you young

groovers. I would hang around, but I've seen more fights than I can eat this holiday. S'laters."

Dave stopped tying his boots. "Er, Georgia, are you all right? Normally, you like a bit of fisticuffs."

I smiled in a sophisticosity-at-all-times sort of way and was about to walk on when Emma said, "I was just talking to Dave about you. I thought your Viking hornpipe dance sounded really groovy. Will you be doing it again at a Stiff Dylans gig? Are you really going to Italy to see Masimo? How very cool. Isn't that cool, Dave? It must be luuurve. When are you off?"

And she was all smiley and nice. Why? Why was she so smiley and nice? Why was her hand on Dave's hair all the time? Did she think it would fall off if she didn't hold it on?

Dave was looking at me. What was I supposed to say?

I was going to say something smart and funny or maybe even sing "O Sole Mio" if my brain entirely dropped out, but I couldn't. There is something about Dave's eyes that makes me tell the truth, so I said, "Well, actually, my cat – well, he's not very well. He was run over and – and I think, I think I will have to cancel my trip and look after him."

Oh, nooooo. I could feel the tears welling up again, I must go. And I walked off really quickly.

At the vet's
5:00 p.m.

Angus is still just lying there. The vet says there is no change and that he thought he would have "gone on" by now. He said it nicely, but I wanted to hit him.

He said, "I'll speak to your mum in the morning and see what she says. You see the thing is, Georgia, it costs an awful lot of money for him to be here and your mum and dad, well – maybe they—"

Walking home

Oh, I am so miserable. I don't know what to do. I can't give up on him, I can't. I wish I had someone to help me.

Lying in my bed
6:30 p.m.

Mum came into my room. Libby is coming home tonight. I said to Mum, "What are we going to tell her? Shall we say, oh, Libby, you know Angus that is your pussycat that you lobe, well, Mummy and Daddy can't be bothered to look after him because he is sick?"

Mum burst into tears. "Oh, Georgia, that is so mean."

She's right actually. I put my arms around her.

"I'm sorry, Mum, I don't mean it."

Bloody hell this is quite literally Heartbreak Hotel. And I am in the sobbing suite again.

9:00 p.m.

Libby is in bed with me. I have read her *Sindyfellow* and *Heidi* twice. Which has turned my brain to soup.

She snuggled down with me and Mr Potato Head (literally a potato with one of her hats on). Gordy came in and leaped on her and started tussling her knees under the covers. She was howling with laughter and hitting Gordy with the potato.

"Huggyhugghoghoghog. Funny pussycat. Get off now." And she just got hold of Gordy around his neck and flung him off the bed. He shook himself and sneezed and growled and she laughed.

"Heggo he laaaikes flying. Snuggle now, Ginger." And she got me in a headlock and started sucking my ear going, "Mmmmmmmmmmmmmm."

After a little while the sucking stopped and she started snoring quietly. I looked at her face in the moonlight; she is such a dear little thing really (when she is unconscious). I didn't want her to ever be sad or upset. I kissed her soft little head. Poo, it smelt of cheese. What does she smear herself with? She stirred in her sleep and put her pudgy arms up in the air. Then she sat up.

"Georgie, where is big pussycat?"

Oh blimey.

I said, "Erm, well, he's in the – kittykat hospital. He's hurt his – paws."

She got out of bed. "Come on, Ginger, let's get him." And she started putting her welligogs on over her pyjamas. She was still half asleep.

I started to say something and she flung Mr Potato at me and started waggling her finger. "Don't you bloody start, you baaaad boy. Get up."

In the end I told her that he would be snoozing and that we would go and get him in the morning and she eventually went to sleep.

Friday August 26th

Libby only went to nursery on condition that I went and got Angus.

I looked at Mum. Mum looked at me. But looking at each other wasn't going to help, was it?

9:00 a.m.
Phone rang. Oh God. What if it's the vet?

If I don't answer it, he can't tell me anything I don't want to know. But...

I answered the phone. It was Dave the Laugh.

"Georgia, what's going on?"

"Oh, Dave, it's Angus, and the vet says, and he's all in his tubes and tongue lolling and even his tail is broken, and Libby said go and get him and she had her welligogs over her jimjams, and I can't bear it."

And I started to cry. Again.

He said, "I'll come round. Cover your nungas up."

At the vet's
10:30 a.m.
Standing in front of the cage looking at Angus with Dave the Laugh.

Dave said, "Blimey. He's a bit bent."

I couldn't stand Angus being in a cage any more. In a

strange place. I said to Dr Beardy, "I have to take him home."

The vet tried to persuade me not to.

I was beginning to feel hysterical. I had to take him. I had to. If he was going to die, I wanted him with me, in his own little basket.

Dave the Laugh was ace. He even called the vet "sir" like he was at Eton.

He said to Dr Beardy, "We understand you have done your very best, sir, but now Georgia wants to take care of him, so we'll just take him home."

The vet said to me in a serious voice, "I'm just warning you that he might wake up violent and demented."

Dave said, "I'm usually in quite a good mood when I wake up, sir." Which very nearly, even in such poonosity, made me laugh.

Dr Beardy said, "I mean Angus."

And Dave said, "Actually, I think you would have needed to know him before, sir."

The vet laughed for once and said, "I did look through my predecessor's notes *vis-à-vis* the, erm, castration operation and there was some suggestion of quite wild behaviour. In fact, the notes did say never to let this cat in the surgery again."

168

Two hours later

When we had got Angus in the house and tucked up, things went a bit awkward. Dave was on the other side of Angus's basket looking at him. And then he looked up. And our heads were very close to each other. He said to me, "Don't cry any more, you'll make your eyes hurt." And he stroked my face.

I looked at him and he looked at me. Uh-oh.

Then he just suddenly stood up and said, "I'd better go, Kittyk – er, Georgia. I'm, well, I'm meeting Emma at six."

I stood up quickly and I smiled, although my mouth felt a bit stiff. I said, "Oh yes, yes, of course, yeah you would. Dave, can I just say – thanks so much, I don't know... I..."

For a second he looked like he was going to give me a bit of a kiss but he stopped and just chucked me under the chin and said, "Remember, I am not God in trousers but merely Dave the biscuit..." And he went.

11:00 p.m.

Angus is in the laundry room in his basket under a big blanket. He hasn't moved or anything for hours. On the way home in the cab he did a little *miaow*. It was just a little *miaow*, but it was something.

He didn't open his eyes or anything. But I think a *miaow* is a good sign.

Saturday August 27th

His eyes open now and again but they are all unfocused like he has really overdosed on catnip. Libby and me are giving him water in a little dropper thing because the vet told us to keep him hydrated.

11:00 p.m.

I have tucked in my charges and am off to beddy byes at last. I truly am a great human being. I hope Baby Jesus is noticing. I may get myself a nurse's uniform tomorrow. Libby is already wearing hers.

What if Angus really is brain-dead or can't walk any more or something? Will I have done the right thing? What if I have to push him around in a cat wheelchair for the rest of his life? I can't see any boyfriend putting up with that.

11:20 p.m.

But I would do it. If he can just come round and know who I am, that will be enough for me.

Sunday August 28th

I went downstairs to look in at Angus and he opened his eyes!!! And let out a really creaky *miaow*.

Hurrah, gadzooks and larks a mercy!!! As Billy Shakespeare and his pals would have said. Thank you, thank you, Baby Jesus!!!

I bent down to the basket and said, "Hello, big furry pally, it's me!" And I put my hand on his face and stroked it. He even purred!!! I started to cry again. Oh well, devil take the hindmost – if you can't have a blubbing fest when your cat has nearly gone to that big cat basket in the sky, when can you have a blubbing fest???

I rushed into the kitchen and opened the fridge. I had got kittykat treats just in case he wanted anything. Cream and everything.

Hey, they should make special-flavoured ice cream for cats called mice cream. Do you get it??? Do you see??? Oh good, I have gone hysterical. Hurrah!!!

I got a little dish of cream and carried it into the laundry room. He was lying there with his bandage over his head and stitches everywhere and his tail strapped up, but his eyes were open. I put my finger in the cream and put it to his mouth. At first he didn't respond, but then his tongue came out and licked off the cream. God, I had forgotten how disgusting his tongue was, it was like being licked by someone with sandpaper on their tongue. Possibly. I'll ask Rosie what it is like snogging someone with sandpaper for a tongue. She probably knows!!!

Hahahahaha. I must be cheered up, my brain is chatting rubbish to itself like normal.

I knew when Angus had had enough cream because he bit my finger quite hard. No damage in the jaw department then!

Phoned the Ace Gang to tell them the news. They are all going round to Jas's house for an all-girl barbecue.

Jas said, "Are you coming to the all-girl barbecue to celebrate?"

I said, "Which of you is going to do the barbecue?"

And Jas said, "Dad is."

"It's not exactly all-girl then, is it, Jas?" But then I thought of Jas's dad and I thought actually...

I can't go though. I'd like to because I haven't seen another human being for days. But I can't bear to leave Angus when he is so poorly.

(I said that to Mum earlier on. "Oh, I wish I had some

human company while I nurse Angus." She said, "I've been here all the time as well." I said, "As I said, I wish I had some human company." And she stropped off to have a bath. That was about two hours ago and she is still in there. I don't know what she does in there for so long; it's vair selfish.)

Jas said, "We're going to give one another manicures and try different make-up. Don't you want to have a go?"

I was tempted but I said, "No, I can't, he's still too poorly, but will you phone and let me know all the goss?"

And Jas said, "Will do, Florrie Nightingale. In fact I'll come round tomorrow in the arvie. I went for a walk with Tom yesterday, it was soooo fab. I'll tell you all about it. We actually saw a red admiral, and they are very rare. I thought it was a sign of hope and—"

I said, "Jas, I think my mum might be coming out of the bathroom and I might be able to get in there for the first time in about a year, so hold that thought about the mothy type thing and—"

"A red admiral is a butterfly actually; moths are—"

"Byeeeeeeeeeeeee."

Good grief, I had nearly stumbled into Voleland by mistake.

Monday August 29th

Woke up and went to check on Angus. Found Gordy sleeping in the cat basket with him. Soooo sweet. Gordy was all curled up beside his dad.

His dad might not be so keen if he knew about Gordy's homosexualist tendencies.

Jas came round and kept me company for the afternoon. We mostly tried different sorts of sexy walking. I practised my beach walk.

Jas said, "Your feet are turning in like a duck."

"Jas, I am doing that on purpose; that is how supermodels walk."

"Is it? Why?"

"Jas, I don't know why, they just do. That is *le* rule. Why do they put their tongue behind their bottom teeth when they smile? I don't know, it is a simple rule. Let us just get on with it."

But Jas had gone off into Jasland. "Anyway, why are you practising your beach walk? You aren't going to go to Pizza-a-gogo land now. Which reminds me, Tom was talking to Dom and Dom said that Masimo had phoned him up and was really glad that you were coming. He wouldn't be if he could see you poncing around like a duck. And also if he knew that you aren't coming anyway."

I stopped for a moment to hit Jas over the head with a pillow.

She did have a point though.

I said, "Jas, will you try that number I have got? I tried it again last night and it was the same Yorkshire bloke. I slammed the phone down, but I bet he knew it was me."

She said, "No."

Which is nice.

9:00 p.m.

I wonder why I haven't heard from Masimo. He must be back from the hills by now. Do they have hills in Rome or do they have hillios?

He is expecting me to arrive any day, so how will he know when to meet me if he doesn't get in touch? Perhaps he has got the humpio because I haven't phoned him.

Phoned Jas. "Please help me find out if I've got the right number for Masimo. Pleasey, please, please."

"I've got a face pack on."

"Well, when you take it off then."

"Then I am doing my cuticles."

I slammed the phone down, she is sooo annoying. Oooooh, what shall I do??? Who might know the number?

Angus started yowling. He's getting a bit bored in his basket of pain now and I have to go and dangle stuff in front of him that he can biff with his nose.

Thirty minutes later

I had a quick mini-break from cat care.

Phoned Rosie. "Rosie, will you get Sven to pop down the snooker hall and see if any of the lads are there and if they have got Masimo's number?"

"Okey-dokey. I'll call you back, *amigo.*"

Forty minutes later

None of the Dylans are in town. Now what shall I do?

Looked in at Angus before I went to bed. Gordy is in the basket, and Naomi and Libby.

She said, "Night night, me sleepin' with big Uggy."

Tuesday August 30th
10:00 a.m.

The Portly One has landed. He leaped out of his robin mobile like he had been to Antarctica instead of pretending to go fishing with Uncle Eddie. I notice he had no fish.

He kissed Mum on the cheek and she seemed a bit shy and not saying much. But at least she said hello and didn't hit him.

Dad went and looked at Angus and was quite shocked, I think. He bent down to the basket and stroked his head and I heard him say, "Poor little chap, you've been in the wars, haven't you?" Quite touching really.

I went into the kitchen and said to Mum, "Hmm, well it seems like—"

At which point we heard from the laundry room, "Bloody hell, you big furry bastard, you nearly had my bloody finger off!!!"

I went on, "It seems like dear Pater is back."

In bed
All quiet on the parent front. They are talking really quietly so that I can't hear them. But Mum did laugh once and I thought I heard some kind of slurping noise. Er, yuck. I hope they were eating jelly.

Midnight

I am eschewing Jas with a firm hand because she is obsessed with her stupid cuticles and wouldn't even help me phone Masimo.

He must phone soon, surely?

Wednesday August 31st

The phone rang. I leaped to get it. It was Dave the Laugh.

"Hi, Gee, how is the Furry One?"

I should have been disappointed that it wasn't Masimo, but to be honest, I had a really warm feeling when I heard Dave's voice.

I said, "He pretended to be asleep and ill, but when Dad put his hand on his nose, I mean Angus's nose not his own nose, because that would be a bit odd even for my dad. Well, when he did, Angus bit it."

Dave laughed, "Brilliant. So you are a bit cheered up?"

I gabbled on. "Yeah, actually it was funny, you would have laughed, but I tried to phone Masimo and I got some bloke called Fat Bob from Yorkshire and he said he couldn't get any decent pickled eggs in Rome!"

Dave said, "Right, so you're off to Rome then?"

I said, "Er, well, I don't want to leave Angus and, well, I—"

Dave said, "Actually, Georgia, I have to run, so I'll see you around. Bye."

Wow, that was a bit brutal. I wonder why he had to run? Maybe Emma had turned up or something. You would think that she could wait for just a minute, wouldn't you? Why did he ring if he didn't really want to speak to me?

How weird.

Why can't everyone just speak English?

Thursday September 1st
8:00 a.m.

Joy unbounded. Angus tried to stand up today!!! And he ate some kittykat food. Libby fed it to him with a "poon" and most of it went in his ear, but hurrah hurrah!!!

To perk him up I put on his favourite tune, "Who let the dogs out?" and did an impromptu disco inferno dance. I did the Viking bison dance and, as a special tribute to his kittykatness, I substituted paw movements for the bison horn bit. I think I am a genius dance-wise!!! And even though Angus just let his tongue loll out and closed his eyes, I can tell that deep down he is secretly thrilled at my tribute dance.

That is what I think.

I have quite literally single-handedly nursed Angus out of danger.

Well, I have had a bit of help.

It was nice of Dave the Laugh to go and get Angus with me.

Vair nice.

Two minutes later

So how come he is Mr Big Pal one minute and the next minute he is too busy to speak to me on the phone?

I hope he doesn't turn into a puppydog boyfriend that just does everything his so-called girlfriend says.

Perhaps he really, really likes Emma. Because maybe she is a top snogger.

Actually, I don't think she is. Her lips are quite thin and I bet that means that there is a bit of toothy exposure during number five on the snogging scale.

Urghh no, I don't want Dave snogging Emma in my brain. I'll hum something to block the picture out.

10:30 a.m.

Phone rang. I said, "Casualty department, Nurse Nicolson speaking."

And a voice said, "*Mi dispiace*, I lookin for Georgia, she for not here?"

Masimo!

I said, "Masimo, it's me, it's me. Georgia. I tried to phone... er phonio you-io and couldn't – I spoke to some people from Yorkshire. I don't know who they were but they were on holiday in Italy and having a lovely time, but – I – oh, it is soooo nice to hear from you."

Masimo was laughing. "Ah, Miss Georgia, you are funny. I am back from ze hills, and I am thinking when you are for to come a Roma. *Mi dispiace*... I am sorry for my English. Now I am with my *famiglia*, it is like I *stupido*... how you say, even more crappio."

I said, "Masimo, well, the thing is, about me coming to Rome, well, my pussycat – you know my..."

Damn, what was the word for cat? Surely it couldn't be cattio?

I said, "My cattio is not well."

He sounded puzzled. "You are not well? Why, what is wrong with you?"

Oh merd-io.

"Not me, my cat. You know, Angus is..."

And I started doing pathetic *miaowing* down the phone. Oh good, I was talking to my Italian Stallion sophisticated boyfriend and pretending to be a cat. Excellent.

In the end I managed to get Masimo to understand. He said, "So you are not for to come for me?"

I felt quite upset, he sounded really sad. And I wanted to see Rome, although I would probably starve to death there, and never get to the lavatory or anything. It had taken me almost all of my life to tell Masimo that Angus was ill. Why can't everyone speak English? Are they just too lazy? I didn't say that though.

Twenty minutes later

We talked and talked. Well, we tried to talk, but people kept coming in to where Masimo was talking to me on the phone and he would shout at them in Pizza-a-gogo-ese. It was all sorts of people – boys, girls, his mum, his dad, aunties, uncles, dogs, and I can't be sure but I think a parrot came in as well.

They certainly seem vair sociable, the Italianos. And quite good-natured. If my family had been in the house when I was

 183

talking to Masimo, it would have been mostly shouting and swearing – and that would have just been Libby.

Then his brother came into the room and Masimo said, "*Cara*, Roberto and I will sing for you a song from the heart."

I started to say, "Well, it's all right, I – you needn't..." But they had already started.

When they finished Masimo said, "It is an old song called 'Volare' and it mean that my love has given me the wings."

Blimey. A bit odd, but that is the romantic Latins for you.

When we said *arrivederci*, Masimo kissed me down the phone. He asked me to do the same. I must say I felt a bit of a prat kissing the phone. But that is transcontinental romance for you.

Five minutes later

I've never had anyone say they love me before. Libby lobes me, that is true, but there is something a bit menacing about the way she says it.

One minute later

And Dave the Laugh kind of said he did. What was it he said when he fished me out of the water in the woods? Oh, yeah. "And that is why I love you."

But he doesn't seem to love me now. In fact, to be frank, he seems to be doing a Jas. Also known as having the humpty with me.

Anyway, shut up, brain. Concentrate on the Luurve God in the hand, not the Dave the Laugh in the bushes.

Ten minutes later
Masimo is going to fly back to Billy Shakespeare land on the 14th. Which is ages away.

Unlike the 12th, the day we go back for more torture and ordure at Stalag 14.

I've said this once and I will say it again. What is the point of school? It is really only to keep the elderly insane off the streets, in my opinion, and to provide shelter for girl-haters.

Ten minutes later
I am quite literally on Cloud 9, luuurve-wise.

One minute later
Tip top of the Love-ometer. I couldn't be happier even if I was a hamster on happy pills scampering up my ladder.

 185

One minute later

The only thing is, though, that I get the hurdy-gurdy knee trembling and wubbish brain whenever I speak to Masimo. He makes me feel shy. And I don't really know what he's like. I mean, when you look at the nub and the gist of the situation, I have in effect only snogged him three times.

Three minutes later

I wonder who I have snogged the most times?

I may have to compose my snogging history until one of my so-called friends can be bothered to phone me up. I am always doing the calling up, so let them make an effort for a change.

Two minutes later

Tragically, my first sexual experience involved incest. My cousin touched me on the leg when we were sharing a room. And then he suggested we play "tickly bears".

I am probably scarred for life mentally, but I don't complain. At least I don't get made to hang out with him now because he has joined the navy. So with a bit of luck he will turn gay.

One minute later
Then there was Peter Dyer, also known as Whelk Boy. Dave the Laugh still can't believe that all us girls actually went round to Whelk Boy's house to learn how to snog. We used to queue up politely outside his door. And he had a timer.

One minute later
In fact Dave the Laugh said, "Now that is a top job. Teaching girls to snog. It is quite literally the Horn come true."

Back to my list.

Next came Mark Big Gob.

One minute later
To tell you the truth, my list is not perking me up much so far. In fact, it is depressing the arse off me. What was I thinking of, snogging Mark Big Gob?

I can't even bear to look at him now. How could I snog him??? I think he must have sort of hypnotised me into doing it. I think I was so mesmerised by the sheer size of his mouth that I was paralysed.

Anyway, it is giving me the droop to think about it, so I will move swiftly on.

Then was it the Sex God? Or did I accidentally snog Dave the Laugh first?

No, I think it was the Sex God because then he said I was too young for him and I used Dave the Laugh as a red herring to make him jealous.

And it was a bit of a surprise because Dave was quite good at snogging.

In fact, very good. He did the lip-nibbling thing, which was quite groovy. But, anyway...

Then it was the Sex God deffo.

Aaah, Robbie. My first love. Funny that you can care so much about someone and then they are just another bloke. Not that I don't care about him. I do. It's just that – oh, I don't know. I hope he is not still so upset. He looked like he was going to say something to me at the footie, until Miss Octopussy Head started asking him to get her a Coke and so on. And then threatening me with torture at Stalag 14.

I can't think about it. I'll get on with my list.

Blimey, then I'm afraid it was the Hornmeister again, encouraging me towards the General Horn. Bad, bad Dave the Laugh...

Then the Sex God again.

Then Dave the Laugh.

Then the Luuurve God.

Then Dave the Laugh again.

I am beginning to see a pattern emerging here. Hmmmm.

One minute later

Of course, I have not included animal snogging, like when Angus accidentally stuck his tongue in my mouth.

Or weird toddler behaviour. Libby snogging my ear. Ditto knees.

Five minutes later

Jas phoned at last. And I was full of coolnosity with her. But she didn't notice because she only wanted to talk about making Tom so fascinated by her that he will forget about going away to college.

I said grumpily, "Well, you can start doing glaciosity right now. You must start eschewing Tom with a firm hand forthwith and lackaday."

She said, "Rightio."

Hmm. Good, that will serve her right. See how she likes not having a boyfriend around.

Ten minutes later

I am on cat patrol because Angus is trying to escape from his basket. I have tucked the blankets around him really tightly so that he can't leap about and spoil all his stitches and so on. In the end I had to clip his lead on and fasten it to the basket.

He's livid.

But he is still a bit weak and after he had yowled a bit he went off to Snoozeland.

When I went to Boboland, tired from my day of constant caring, I said to Mum, "You should try caring, Mum. It's vair vair tiring."

Friday September 2nd
Up at the crack of 10:30 a.m.

Angus is getting stronger and more mad every day. He hates being in his basket. And he has chewed through his lead. I'm going to have to get him a metal one. He is the Arnold Schwarzenegger of cat land.

Twenty minutes later

I can't stand the sound of moaning and miaowing and yowling any more. Maybe if I take him outdoors, he will calm down a bit. Besides which, he has eaten so much of his basket, it is practically just a pile of old sticks.

11:00 a.m.

Jas came round to report on her boy entrancing skills *vis-à-vis* Hunky.

I am preparing myself to forgive her, just to pass the time actually.

I said, "Right, what did you say when you last saw him?"

She did a bit of fringe fiddling and then said, "Hmmm, I said, see you later."

I said, "Right, that's good, very good, nice and vague, give him time to wonder what you have been up to and so on. When did you last see him?"

She did more fringe-fiddling and thinking then she said, "Erm, let me see – erm, it was about half an hour ago."

"Half an hour ago! Jas, you are not as such getting this, are you? You are officially giving him space so he can come pinging back like an elastic band. Seeing him half an hour ago is not having space; that is seeing him all the time."

"I like to see him."

"That is as maybe, but it is not the key to entrancement."

"What is then?"

"You must be more mysterious and unavailable. You must gird your loins and display glaciosity and so on. You must make him jealous."

"Why?"

"Because jealous is good *vis-à-vis* entrancementosity."

"How do I make him jealous? Shall I say I found some unusual molluscs and not show them to him?"

"No. I am not talking about nature, I am talking about the game of luuurve. You have to flirt with other blokey fandangos."

"How do you mean?"

"I mean, you flirt with other blokey fandangos."

"That is all very well for you, Georgia. You are inclined to thrust your red bottom about, but it is against my nature."

Oh, she is soooo annoying.

In the end I got her to agree that she will practise flirting with other boys. And she will play Tom at his own gamey and win. She said, "Right, I'm going to start now. I am practising glaciosity. This is me being unavailable." And she tilted her nose up and flicked her fringe.

"No, Jas, that is just you looking stupid in my house

where Tom can't even see you. You have to do something that he will notice."

She had a bit of a think and then said, "Right, I'm going to phone him and say that I think he's right that we should have more space and that I need more space actually, because he has been my only one and only. And that I will see him when I have a spare moment."

"Good, that is good, Jas."

She went off to phone him and I started rooting around in the garage for a cat transporter. I hope I don't get attacked by bluebottles. Usually when dad has been fishing he leaves his maggots in their little maggot home thing, forgets about them and they turn into huge bluebottles. I peered in. No menacing humming going on – so – now then, what can I put Angus in as a sort of cat wheelchair? Aha!!! Libby's old pushchair!!! Perfect.

Four minutes later

Jas came back looking a bit flushed. I was trying to work the straps out on the pushchair and she was flicking her fringe around like a madwoman.

She said, "Well, that's done. I've told him. I said I was

 193

having a bit of space and that he should have a bit of space. And he said OK. Which is a bit weird. What do you think he meant by OK?"

I said, "I think he meant OK. Now, where is the bit that clicks into the buckle?"

"Anyway, whatever he means, I'm quite looking forward to a bit of freedom. You know, trying out my entrancing skills and so on. What is the special entrancing walk thingy?"

I showed her the hip hip wiggle wiggle hip hip thing. And also did a bit of flicky hair.

Two minutes later
She managed the hip hip wiggle wiggle thing, but when she tried to incorporate flicky hair at the same time, she banged into a wall.

Ten minutes later
We carried Angus out to the driveway in the washing-up bowl. We tried to lift the cat basket up, but the bottom just fell out and Angus was yowling like a cat who has just crashed to the floor out of its basket.

Both of us were wearing gardening gloves. I'd like to say

that Angus was really looking forward to his little outing and in his catty way appreciated what we were doing for him, but the spitting and pooing would suggest otherwise.

I said to Jas as we shoved him down the drive in the pushchair, "You have to be cruel to be kind. Some things in life are not pleasant, but they have to be done. For instance, German and maths. And, well, school. I can't believe the holidays have gone so quickly and we are being forced back into the torture chamber of life."

Jas said, "I'm quite looking forward to it now. We're doing *Romeo and Juliet* in English. I wonder if I will get a part like I did in last year's production. You know, I really felt that I got into the Lady M part. It took quite a lot out of me."

I said, "It took quite a lot out of me."

But she had gone off into Jasland. Is it likely that she will be cast as Juliet? Because that is what she is thinking. Whoever heard of a Juliet with a stupid flicky fringe and an obsession with owls? Billy Shakespeare didn't write, "Hark what owl through yonder window breaks?"

Five minutes later
Angus is nicely strapped into the pushchair. I have put a

 195

little blankin over him and tucked a couple of sausages under his armpit so he can reach them for a nibble.

As we wheeled Angus out of our gate Mr and Mrs Next Door were coming back from walkies with the Prat brothers. They were looking unusually unusual today in matching pink collars. And the poodles looked ridiculous too!!! Hahahaha, did you see what I did there? Oh, nevermind.

Mr Next Door looked at us wheeling Angus along and said, "He's not dead then?" And he didn't say it in a pleased way.

Naomi followed us for a while doing that mad high-pitched thing that nutcase Burmese cats do. But then, when she reached the end of the road, the big black manky cat was lurking around by the dustbins and she caught his eye. Angus went ballisticisimus when he saw Manky and tried to bite through his straps. I started pushing the pushchair really quickly. Naomi is an appalling tart; she just lay down in the road and started squiggling around on her back, letting her womanly parts run wild and free.

How disgusting. I said to Jas, "Put your hand over Angus's eyes."

Jas said, "Er, no, because I'm not mad and I don't want it bitten off."

It's awful really. Poor crippled Angus seeing his woman offering herself to other (manky) men.

I started jogging along with the pushchair, but I hadn't got my specially reinforced sports nunga-nunga holder on, so I had to stop as there was a bit of a danger of uncontrollable bounce basooma-wise.

Four minutes later

We ambled along towards the park. It was quite a nice day. I put a sun bonnet on Angus because there are some baldy patches on his head where the stitches are and he might have got sunburn. I thought he looked quite cute but he didn't agree and was trying to biff me with his big paw.

When he was under his blankin and with his hat over his face, you couldn't really tell he was a cat. I said to Jas, "It would be quite funny if people actually thought he was a baby. Then they might bend down to say 'Aaaahhh' and see his mad furry face staring out at them. And that would be a hoot and a half."

Jas said, "Yeah, groovy." But she didn't mean it because I could tell she was concentrating on practising doing wiggle wiggle, hip hip, flicky hair, flicky hair, fall off pavement etc.

In the end, Angus made such a racket and the bonnet fell down over his eyes, so I took it off. I told Jas she could wear it to keep her fringe in check but she didn't want to. She is quite literally a fun-free zone.

I said to Jas, "I bet you that the teachers are actually looking forward to going back to Stalag 14 because they have no lives. I bet Slim already has her knickers laid out ready to go. Hawkeye will be practising shouting."

Jas said, "Oh, I meant to tell you something. Tom told me goss about Robbie and Wet Lindsay."

"Jas, I told you not to do any earwigging *vis-à-vis* Droopy Knickers."

"I didn't do earwigging. Tom just brought it up. Apparently Wet Lindsay goes round to Tom's mum and dad's all the time. Even when neither of the boys are there. She just goes and hangs out with the parents. How sad is that? And they get on really well. So Tom asked Robbie what was going on, was she like the official girlfriend etc. and Robbie said, and I quote, 'Well, it's nice to have someone who is sort of ordinary around and who really likes me.' Oh, and he also said that she bakes him cakes."

I just looked at Jas. "What sort of person bakes cakes for boys?"

Jas said, "Well, I made a lemon drizzle cake for Tom when we went camping and—"

"OK, let me put this another way, what sort of twit besides your good self makes cakes for boys? It is tremendously sad and odd. It doesn't say one word about cake baking in my *How to Make Any Twit Fall in Love with You* book and it says some pretty bloody strange things, I can tell you."

Of course, for no apparent reason, Jas hit number seven on the having-the-hump scale. (Number seven is, of course, walking on ahead, one of Jas's specialities).

I said, "Jazzy, don't be silly. I bet Tom luuurved your drizzley cake. It's just odd for Wet Lindsay to do it, isn't it? She's not exactly a domestic, is she? It's not like her to do anything for anyone else, is it? Is it, little pally? I bet even Tommy wommy said that it was a bit odd, didn't he?"

Jas didn't want to say, but she couldn't help it. She said, "Well, actually, he did say he thought that she was, like, a bit insincere and that she was trapping Robbie by being nice."

Hmmm. That has made me feel a bit guilty about Robbie. If he was on the rebound because I had eschewed him with a firm hand, I had sort of made him go back out with the octopussy prat of the century. It was bad enough having him cry in front of me, but for him to then be driven into her no-forehead world was awful. I didn't want him to be with Lindsay because of me. Maybe I would have to save him from her somehow.

Twelve minutes later

We were wheeling Angus along in the park singing "Always Look on the Bright Side of Life" quite loudly to cheer him up (he was yowling along to the chorus, I like to think) when round the corner of the loos came Dave the Laugh and Emma, and Tom and a friend of Emma's called Nancy. They were laughing together.

Dave saw us first and he came over and bent down to look at Angus. "Wow, you dancer! Attaboy. You're de man!!!"

He said it in a sort of admiring way and I felt really proud of Angus. He had come back from the edge of the heavenly cat basket in the sky like supercat. And it was nice to see Dave. He looked very cool in a class shirt and he looked up and winked at me – then spoiled the moment by saying, "Emma, come and have a look at Angus; he is the kiddie."

Emma came trolling across all girlie. "Ooooh, isn't he cute?"

I should have warned her not to put her face too near Angus but, well, that is the law of nature. It's only cat spit, after all. You would have thought that it was viper juice, the way she carried on. She went scampering off into the ladies' loos and Nancy went with her.

Jas had not said a word since she saw Tom. She had gone very, very red, even for her, that is how red she was.

Tom said, "I just bumped into Dave and the girls at the snooker hall..."

Jas said, "Tom, what you do is really your business. Come on, Gee, we don't want to keep the gang waiting." And she actually said to Tom, "S'laters. Maybe bell you sometime." Has she finally snapped?

I followed after her with the pushchair, leaving Tom and Dave looking at us.

When we got round the corner, Jas burst into tears.

"How can he just go and get off with some other girl, just like that? It's only half an hour since I said he could be free."

I said, "Well, it says in my *How to Make Any Twit Fall in Love with You* book that boys don't like feeling bad, so they get another girl really quickly."

Jas said, "That's awful. What's the point of seeing anyone then or caring about boys at all?"

I said, "Well, there is some good news."

"What?"

"Well, it says that they get another girl really quickly and it is usually a disaster. And they remain frozen emotionally for the rest of their lives, so that's good, isn't it?"

But she didn't cheer up as such.

Saturday September 3rd
9:00 a.m.

Jas phoned. She said, "Tom came round and said that there was nothing going on with Nancy. He just bumped into them and they had a bit of a kick around with the other lads in the park and the girls watched. And, anyway, Nancy has got a boyfriend. She is just, like, Emma's best mate."

I said, "What did you say?"

"Well, I remembered, you know, about the glaciosity and so on. And I said, 'I suppose that when you are having space you can't always ask what someone is doing and so on but we can be friendly to each other.'"

I was amazed. I said, "Jas, my little matey, that is almost quite good tactics. You are not only displaying glaciosity, you are also incidentally displaying maturiosity as well. *Muchos buenos,* as our Pizza-a-gogo friends might say."

Then she spoiled it. "I miss him though."

I said, "Go cuddle your owls and be brave."

She said, "Am I allowed to snog him if he comes round?"

I said, "No, he has to go off and then ping back. You can't do the pinging first. It is not in the book."

Tuesday September 6th

Six days to Stalag 14. God help us one and all. But on the bright side the Luuurve God comes back in eight days!!! I am keeping up my grooming and plucking so that I do not have to do it all in one go. I am ruthless with any stray hairs. Also I am a lurker-free zone. I just wish I could find some tan stuff that makes my legs not so paley, but not orange like last time. Anyway, it doesn't really matter because we will be back in tights for school.

4:00 p.m.

Angus went for his first walk today. I put him on top of the dividing wall so that he could see the Prat Poodles. They usually give him *joie de vivre* and so on. His tail is still all bandaged up but his stitches come out next week and he is eating A LOT.

I popped him up there but he still seemed a bit wobbly on his old cat pins. He wobbled up and down once or twice and then crashed off over the wall into Mr and Mrs Next Door's garden. I clambered up and looked down, and he was lying in the cabbage patch. He did that silent *miaowing* thing and then got to his paws again. He started walking and then careered off into a bush. Then he got up again, walked for a few paces and crashed into the lawnmower. Oh noooo, perhaps he really did have brain damage.

I leaped down into Next Door's garden to rescue my little pally. The Next Doors were out, so the coast was clear apart from the heavily permed guardey dogs, Snowy and Whitey. They were chained to their kennel, probably to stop them larking about and getting their stupid fur all muddy. And they were yapping like billio.

I said in a Liverpool accent, "Calm down, calm down," and picked up Angus. He didn't like being picked up and struggled around. As a treat I took him quite near the Prat brothers and he gave them both a big swipe with his paw around the snout.

I took him out through the gate because I didn't think I could manage the wall and Angus the mad cat.

Ooooooh, please don't let him be a backward cat. I didn't

want to have to push him around in his pussycat wheelchair for the rest of my life.

I told Mum what had happened and she said why didn't I ring the vet, Dr Beardy.

What if he said that Angus was like a turnip cat? Would I look after him even if he was dim and didn't know how to fight any more? And started liking the Prat brothers?

Five minutes later
Yes, I would. I love him and I will look after him no matter what happens. He is my furry soul pal.

Wednesday September 7th
Amazingly, Dad was quite sympathetic *vis-à-vis* Angus being an idiot cat and said he would drive me to the vet's when he got back from work.

At the vet's
5:30 p.m.
The vet looked all beardy and serious when I told him about Angus crashing about and maybe being backward. He looked in Angus's ears and eyes and so on. Then he put him up on his table

and let him walk about. Angus took two steps and then immediately fell off the table. He tried to leap up on to it again and missed and crash-landed into my lap. Which he then fell off.

It was so sad. He had been the king of leaping and balancing. His days of riding the Prat brothers around like little horsies were over. I could feel my eyes filling up.

Dr Beardy said, "It's his tail. He can't balance properly while it's all bandaged up. He'll be OK when the bandage comes off."

Oh, Allah be praised!!!

(Er, sorry about that, Baby Jesus. I don't know why I came over a bit Muslim then, but we are all in the same cosmic gang after all. Clearly I have my favourite, which is Baby Jesus, but generally I am a fan of the whole caboodle. In case any of them are also omnipotent like Big G.)

Back home

Angus has just crashed into the cat flap which he was trying to get through. Oh, I am so happy. I told Jas on the phone.

She went, "Ahuhu-ahuh." But not in a caring and listening way.

Then she said, "I don't know how you manage without a boyfriend. Who do you tell stuff to?"

I said, "Jas, I tell stuff to my little pallies, like you. Anyway, can I stop you before you go off on a Moaning for Britain campaign? I am going to ring the Ace Gang and we can have a joint celebration day for the recovery of Angus and also the reinvention of – glove animal!!!"

"Oh no."

"Oh yes."

"Oh no."

"Oh yes."

"Oh no."

"Jas, this is lots of fun chatting with you and so on – but we are meeting at mine in half an hour, so you had better dash. Pip pip."

Round at mine

I have made all of the gang coffee and Jammy Dodgers as we need nourishment to prepare us for the beginning of another term at Stalag 14.

Two hours later

My ribs are hurting from laughing. I had forgotten how much fun you can get out of a beret and a pair of gloves. It was Rosie's impression of Inspector Glove Animal of the Yard that made me laugh the most. She put on the beret and pinned the gloves underneath it as ears, and then popped her beard on and started puffing on her pipe.

It was vair vair *amusant*. I said, "I think Hawkeye will appreciate the creativitinosity that we have brought to what is in fact a boring old beret."

Jas said, "She won't appreciate it; she will just give us immediate detention."

I looked at her with my eyebrows raised. "Jas, I hope you are not being the bucket-of-cold-water girl."

Jas was going on in rambling mode. "Well, it's so silly."

Rosie went over to her and took out her pipe. "Jas, are you suggesting that I look silly?"

Oh, I laughed.

To release our girlish high spirits we danced around to loud music in my bedroom and then we lay down panting on the bed.

Ellen is going on a proper second date with Declan, and Rollo bought Jools her very own rattle for supporting him at his footie matches. She is secretly thrilled, I think, although she said she would rather have had chocolates and lip gloss.

Sunday September 11th
In bed
11:30 p.m.

My bedroom is a Libby-free zone. I've got Stalag 14 tomorrow and I want to be in tip-top condition to face the Hitler Youth (prefects). And General Fascists (staff). And the Lesbians (Miss Stamp). And other assorted loons (Herr Kamyer, Elvis, Miss Wilson, Slim our beloved huge headmistress and – well, everyone else there really).

Hark! What owl through yonder window breaks?

Monday September 12th
7:00 a.m.
Oh, I can't believe the hols are over and it is back to long dark hours of boredom and – er... that's it. Still, it's now only two days until Masimo gets back. Yarooooo!!!!

In the bathroom
7:25 a.m.
I was just about to wash my face with the special face-washing soap when I realised it wasn't there. How am I

supposed to cleanse and tone etc. if people keep moving my soap? I went into the kitchen and said to Mum, "Have you been using my special soap, which is specially mine especially for me?"

She didn't even look round. "No."

I looked in at Angus. He and Gordy were in the same basket and they were both frothing at the mouth.

7:40 a.m.
Why would a cat eat soap? Why?

8:30 a.m.
Walking really, really slowly up the hill towards Hell.

Jas hasn't phoned Tom and he has phoned her twice and she has pretended that she isn't in.

I said, just to check, "Er, Jas, you know how you pretended that you weren't in? Well, you didn't answer the phone and say 'I'm not in', did you?"

She hit me over the head with her rucky, which was a bit violent, I think. It is as well I luuurve her.

We are not doing glove animal today, we are keeping the element of surprise. Hawkeye and the Hitler Youth will be on high alert at the moment. All full of energy after the summer break. All pepped up for mass brutality and girl hating so we are going to lull them into a false sense of security by being good this week. And then going all out headgear-wise next week.

8:38 a.m.
The fascist regime has already started. As we came through the school gates Hawkeye was there like a guard dog and she had a tape measure!! Honestly! She was making sure that our skirts were an inch below the knee. Anyone who had turned over their skirt at the waist was given an immediate reprimand for their trouble. I may write to my MP or the European King or whatever.

Fortunately, I knew Hawkeye would be picking on me (as she has a specially developed hating muscle all for me), so I had pulled my skirt down over my knees once we were in sight of Stalag 14's perimeter fence.

Melanie Griffiths, world renowned for her enormous out of control nungas, was just ahead of me and Hawkeye pounced. Fair enough because Melanie's skirt was practically up her bum-oley.

Hawkeye had a nervy spaz attack: "Melanie, I would have expected better from you and, frankly, with your shape, you would do well to go for the longer look anyway."

I said to Jas, "Actually, I don't think that Melanie has rolled her skirt up. I think that her arse has grown and that has lifted the hemline."

As we shuffled off to hang our coats up I grumbled to the rest of the gang, "I bet they don't have people measuring bloody skirts in schools in Pizza-a-gogo land. I bet they don't even wear skirts at schools there, they are so liberal. I bet they wear fur thongs or leatherette hotpants."

Actually, I hope they don't. Masimo might quite like that. Oooohhhh, I can't wait for him to come back.

Assembly

Oh, hello to the wonderful world of mass boredom and *merde*. Wet Lindsay and her sidefool, Astonishingly Dull Monica, were lurking around on prefect duty. They love frightening the first formers, telling them their shoes are wrongly laced up and so on.

Wet Lindsay looked at me and said something to ADM and they both laughed. I didn't care though; I have an

Italian Luuurve God as a boyfriend. And, more importantly, I have got a forehead.

We were just queuing up to go through the doors into the main hall and listen to Slim, our revered headmistress, bore for England when the two Little Titches came bounding up. I haven't seen the Titches, also known as Dave the Laugh's fan club, since the last Stiff Dylans gig. They were all flushed and excited and the (slightly) less titchy one said to me, "Hello... hello, miss. We've got new trainers. We'll show you them later. And we saw Dave the Laugh yesterday at the shopping centre. He went into Boots and we followed him and he was getting some moisturiser and then we asked him for his autograph and he signed my maths book. He put three kisses and a drawing of a monkey."

Wet Lindsay shouted out, "You two lower-school girls get back in line and stop talking. Georgia Nicolson, take a reprimand for encouraging the younger girls to break school rules."

What, what? I had got a reprimand for standing in line while some tiny nutcases told me about their new shoes. Where was the justice in that?

God, I hate her. In fact, she has made me deffo decide to split her and Robbie up somehow. It is my civic duty. Also, if I can accidentally on purpose bend her stupid bendy stick-insecty legs round her neck, I will most certainly take the opportunity.

As we shuffled to our places I whispered to Jas out of the corner of my mouth, "I hate her. She is definitely as dead as a dead thing on dead tablets. Also, forgive me if I am right, but Dave the Laugh seems to have acquired his own personal stalkers."

Fifteen minutes later

Ro Ro really made me laugh during prayers because she dug me in the ribs and when I looked at her she had on those comedy glasses that have no lenses but do have a false nose with big black eyebrows on. I couldn't stop laughing and then she did it to the rest of the gang, so we had group shoulder heaving. I managed to pull myself together for the final amen.

I could see Wet Lindsay looking over our way, but she could only see Rosie from the side so she didn't get the full bushy eyebrow effect, otherwise it would have been detention all round. What larks!

Also the hymn was a top opportunity for "pants" work. The words were, "I long for you Lord as the deer PANTS for the rain."

 215

The volume went up about a million when we sang "pants".

Four minutes later

Oh, go on a bit, why don't you, Slim. "Blah blah blah, visitors saying girls looked like prostitutes wearing short skirts, make-up etc etc... all girls going to be hung, drawn and quartered if they don't keep to school dress codes, blah blah. A lady does not show her knickers underneath her skirt."

Oh, I am so bored. Slim had worked herself up into such a state that I thought her chins were going to drop off. Also, vis-à-vis fashion etc. I am not sure that I would wear an orange dress if I were eighty-four stone. She must get them specially made. By a sadist.

Then she said, "Well girls, now let us pass on to more pleasant matters. As you know, before the summer holidays Year Eleven were lucky enough to be taken on a camping trip by Herr Kamyer and Miss Wilson. I gather that they had a marvellous time. Is that true, Year Eleven?"

Me and Rosie and the gang were murmuring, "Yes, oh yes. Are you mad? Yes, yes, cheese and onion," and rubbish, but so that you couldn't really hear it. Only Jas and her sad mates were shouting stuff like, "It was great."

Bloody swotty voley knicker types.

Then Slim asked Herr Kamyer and Miss Wilson to come up to the stage. Miss Wilson looked like she was wearing her pre-Christmas cardigan. I swear, it had reindeers on it. And Herr Kamyer had on a tweed suit and an unusual tie (knitted) and his trousers hovered proudly at ankle level, revealing attractive matching socks.

Good grief. I whispered to Jools, "It's lovely young love, isn't it?" She just looked at me.

Herr Kamyer went first. He said, "Vell, ve had ze very gut time viz the fun and larfs. Didn't ve, girls?"

We all went, "Whatever, mumble mumble."

Miss Wilson took over the dithering baton then. "It was most enjoyable. During the day we drew interesting sketches of the varied wildlife and explored our environs."

Rosie went, "Oo-er," which nearly made me wet myself but no one else heard.

Miss Wilson was back in the exciting world of tents and voles, rambling on. "But the evenings were in many ways the best times, we made our own entertainment."

Slim interrupted, "Always the most enjoyable."

Miss Wilson said, "Indeed."

God, it was like a hideous teacher love-in.

Then Herr Kamyer got the giddygoat and started being enthusiastic. "Yah, ve played some of the games I haf played when I was camping in ze Black Forest. We did the shadow animals game and Miss Vilson sang mit der girls and made ze vair *gut spangleferkel.*"

Oh dear God, I knew it wouldn't be long before we were back on the sausage trail.

Actually, I didn't mind idling time away with sausages and mad Germans because we had French first lesson, and I wanted to avoid Madame Slack for as long as I could because she hates me.

As Herr Kamyer and Miss Wilson both dithered and fell down the stairs from the stage, Slim said something scary.

"Well, I am sure there will be many more expeditions and excitements in the coming terms. Also I think it would be very nice for the whole school to share in the memories of the trip, and so I have suggested that Miss Wilson run an art project with Year Eleven. It will be lovely for them to bring their paintings and sculptures and so on of their feelings and experiences of the camping trip and put them on display here in the main hall."

Rosie whispered to me, "Will you be bringing the sculpture of your snogging session with Dave the Laugh into the main hall?"

I looked at her cross-eyed and said, "I wonder if Miss Wilson will be re-enacting, through the magic of dance, her marvellous standing in a field in the nuddy-pants scenario?"

French

I have *dit* this many times and I will *dite* it again, *qu'est ce que c'est le point de français*?

I've been to *le* gay Paree, I have experienced *le* mime, I have danced *sur le pont* d'Avignon and even (as Jools reminded me) done my world-famous impression of the Hunchback of Notre Dame outside Notre Dame. But I will not be going again.

This is *moi* point. I go out with an Italian Luuurve God and there is no point in going to France except for cheese. And I do not *aime* cheese, so there you are.

Madame Slack was just waiting to give me a good verbal thrashing, and when I innocently said in our conversation section that *"Je préfère l'Italie pour mes vacances and pour*

l'amour. Je n'aime pas le fromage. Merci. Au revoir." Madame Slack said, "Ah well, *je préfère les étudiants qui ne sommes pas des idiots – mais c'est la vie. Prenez vous le reprimand."*

Bloody hell, two reprimands and I haven't even had my break-time cheesy wotsits.

Lunchtime

I wonder why Dave the Laugh was buying moisturiser from Boots? Perhaps he is on the turn. I may say that to him when I see him. I may say, "Dave, your skin is sooo soft and smooth. Are you on the turn?"

Not that I will be seeing him.

Probably.

German

Rosie has been looking in her new slang book, *German for Fools.* She said to Herr Kamyer, "In my new dictionary it says that a kiss lasting over three minutes is *abscheidskuss."*

Herr Kamyer quite literally went red all over. And I could clearly see his ankles, so I am sure about this.

He started, "Well, yes, but this language is for slang, and of course one would not say... erm—"

Rosie said helpfully, "*Abscheidskuss?*"

German is quite literally comedy magic.

Five minutes later

Wee is *pipi*.

One minute later

And to poo is *krappe*. Hahahaha.

Still incarcerated in Stalag 14
Afternoon break

Going to school is like going through life backwards in time.

I said to the Ace Gang, "Did you see Miss Wilson choking on her fizzy orange when Herr Kamyer walked past her and asked her if she was wearing a new blouse? She luuurves him. She wants him baaaad. He is quite literally a babe magnet."

Rosie looked up "babe magnet" in the *German for Fools* book. She said, "Oh *ja*, he is a *Traum*boy."

Jools said, "When does Masimo get back?"

I said, "He said the fourteenth."

Ellen said, "What time, I mean, did he say s'later or 'give you a bell' or will he like give you a bell or will you give him a bell?"

We looked at her.

It is true though. He didn't say when exactly he would be back. I don't know what time he will be arriving, morning, afternoon or night. Which means essentially I will be on high alert and heavily made up for twenty-four hours a day. And even then he might not call me until the next day. He might have jet lag.

One minute later

I will have to go to bed fully made up and dressed in case he pops round unexpectedly.

One minute later

I have just had a spontaneous pucker up.

Bell went

As we were scampering back for English (double bubble), I had one of my many ideas of geniosity. I said, "I know what we can do to stop Herr Kamyer from making us do stuff. Let us get him to correct our German translation of the snogging system. That I will be doing during blodge."

English

Miss Wilson announced that we are indeedy going to be doing a school production of *Rom and Jule* this term. And that because of the massive success of MacUseless, we are going to join forces with the boys' school again. They are going to be our "technical support". Which in Dave the Laugh's case means he switches all the lights off and people fall off the stage. Yarroooo!!!

We started yelling out, "Oh joy unbounded!" "Three cheers for merrie England and all who sail in her!" "Poop poop!" "For she's a jolly good fellow!" until I thought Miss Wilson's bob would explode.

She was slightly losing her rag and said, "Now, girls, settle down. I know that it is very thrilling but – Rosie, get off your desk and please put your beard away."

Rosie looked surprised. "But I am getting in character, Miss Wilson. This is an Elizabethan beard, specially knitted by some old bloke in tights many moons ago."

Eventually Miss Wilson was able to say that auditions were to take place on Wednesday in the main hall and that we were to read the text and think about what parts we might like to play.

Nauseating P. Green asked if there was a dog in it. She has never quite got over playing the dog in *Peter Pan*. Miss Wilson said, "No, there is no dog in *Romeo and Juliet*. It is a tragedy."

I said, "You can say that again, Miss Wilson, because Pamela is top at fetching sticks and begging."

We laughed and started muttering "Prithee, prithee, prithee!" and doing pretendy beard stroking every time Miss Wilson started describing the plot of *Rom and Jule*.

After about ten minutes the classroom door banged open. Slim came jelloiding in, shouting and wobbling at the same time, telling us that we were making too much noise and being silly. If we didn't all want to stay behind for detention on our first day back, we should shut up. Ramble ramble, wobble wobble etc.

Charming.

I said to the Ace Gang quietly, "You show a bit of enthusiasm for the Bird of Avon, our greatest old bloke in tights, and this is what you get for your trouble."

And they wonder why the youth of today doesn't learn nuffink.

4:00 p.m.

Ambling out of the science block after the last bell. God, how many years have I been in blodge learning how to bamboozle my epiglottis?

As we rounded the corner towards the main building I saw Wet Lindsay dashing across to the sixth-form common room. She wasn't wearing her uniform; she had on a short dress that showed off her knobbly knees to perfection. She glared at me as she went past, and she was undoing her stupid hair from its stupid ponytail.

I said, "That's a nice dress, Lindsay. Who went to the fitting for it?"

She just gave me two fingers.

I said to Rosie, "She's a lovely example to us all, isn't she?"

4:15 p.m.

Walking across the playground I noticed Robbie sitting on his new (quite cool) scooter on the road by the gates. Most of the girls were getting all girlish and swishing their hair about as they passed him by. He saw me. (Damn, I wish I had put some make-up on!!! I must suck my nose in and smile in an ad hoc and cool way.) He has got really nice eyes and I could

 225

still picture him the day that I told him about me and Masimo and he had let a little tear out of his eye. Actually, considering that he and I only saw each other for a short time, we had packed in an awful lot of blubbing one way and another. We had quite literally spent most of our possible snogging time at Heartbreak Hotel.

Ah, well.

He smiled sort of sadly at me as I got near him. I smiled back. He is very good looking.

He said, "All right, Georgia?"

I said, "Yeah, fine, alrighty as two alrighty things. And you?"

He said, "Yeah, cool, things are you know, er, cool. I'm guesting at the next Stiff Dylans gig... Are... will you be coming? You know with your... er... your—"

At that moment I got a sharp prod in my bum. Owwwww buggery oww. I had been stabbed in my bum-oley. I looked round into the smiling face of Wet Lindsay. Wet Lindsay and her umbrella.

Wet Lindsay said, "Hi, Robbie, ready to go, hon?"

She got on the back of his scooter and while he couldn't see her she was mouthing at me, "You are so dead meat."

Robbie fired up his scooter and said, "See you around,

Georgia." And they roared off.

I watched them and Lindsay turned round and put her finger across her throat, meaning that I was indeedy dead meat.

I rubbed my bum. I would probably have a bruise there and I had only just recovered from my last bum-oley injury.

I grumbled to the others, "She is such a bitch. I can't believe he is falling for it AGAIN. It makes me think he is a bit half-witted.

Jas said, "Remember what you told me about boys getting someone else really quickly when they are upset? Well, maybe you have driven him into the arms of the Stick Insect Octopussy girl. S'laters."

Yep, it looks like I am going to have to make him dump her somehow. I wonder if she still wears those false nunga-nunga increasers?

Five minutes later

Jas has gone a different way home in case Tom is around. Then he will wonder where she is and she will have become entrancing to him.

As I have already been caught without make-up by an ex, I am taking no chances. We nipped into the tarts' wardrobe

227

in the park and we applied mascara, lippy and so on. And I did a bit of hair-bounceability work. (I put my head upside down under the hot-air hand-dryer.) Rolled my skirt over and took off my tie, and *voilà*!!! Georgia the callous sophisticate rides again with her Ace Gang (minus Wise Woman of the Forest)!!

Funnily enough, it was just as well we had done preparation because as we started walking down the hill, Dave the Laugh caught us up. He was with Declan, Edward and Rollo. Ellen, Mabs and Jools went into giggling-gertie mode and sort of lagged back with their "boyfriends", so it was just me and Dave and Rosie.

He linked up with us and said, "Be gentle with me, girls."

Awwww.

I told Dave about the *Rom and Jule* fiasco and he said, "Excellent, excellent. Many comedy opportunities in the tights department there then." He also said he had some kittykat treats for Angus.

Awwww.

As we got to the edge of the park we heard a lot of shouting. The Blunder Boys. Yippee. They saw Dave and gave him the finger. Then Oscar came looming along with his tragic jeans and no belt and one of the spoons yelled, "Wedgie!!!" And two of them got hold of Oscar and pulled down his jeans so that his Thomas the Tank Engine kecks were exposed to the world. Mark Big Gob grabbed the top of Oscar's underpants and lifted him off his feet. He was just dangling there, literally held up by his undercrackers.

Quite, quite mind-bogglingly weird.

Dave was nodding and said, "Excellent work."

We walked on and I said, "Erm, Dave, as you are world expert on the weirdness that is boydom, can you just explain what that was about?"

Dave said, "A wedgie is when the underpants are pulled sharply upward from behind, so that they go tightly up the victim's bum-oley."

We just looked at him.

He went on. "The ultimate is, of course, the atomic wedgie, when you attempt to get the victim's pants over their head."

I said goodbye to Rosie and Dave the Laugh at my turn-off and he and Rosie went off together. Dave looked back at me while he walked backwards. He said, "S'later, you cheeky minx!"

I watched them as they went off. They were laughing and

 229

then did a bit of spontaneous "Let's go down the disco" dancing.

I sort of wished we could have hung round together some more. I really laugh when I am with Dave.

Ah, well.

In my bedroom
If my brain keeps adding up the minutes till Masimo might be back, I'll go mad. I am going to keep my mind (well, what there is left of it) occupied by doing (and I never thought the day would come when I would say this) my homework.

Two minutes later
Now, here we go – *Rom and Jule.*

Two hours later
Bloody hell, Billy Shakespeare can be depressing. *Rom and Jule* is not what you would call a megalarf. Mostly it is just fighting, a bit of underage snogging, more fighting, and then some mad bint who calls herself a nurse and makes useless jokes about sex.

For the hilarious side-splitting finale, Rom and Jule pretend to commit suicide and then they actually do commit suicide.

Two minutes later

I know how they feel – it's double physics tomorrow.

Midnight

If Masimo gets back at nine p.m. that makes it 7020 minutes to wait. Or maybe if he comes back at two p.m. that makes it 6600 minutes. Is there a time difference between here and Italy? Ooooooh I can't sleep. What can I do? It's too early to start my make-up routine. Angus might lick it off in the night.

Two minutes later

I know, I will use the *German for Fools* book that I have borrowed from Ro Ro and finish translating the snogging scale for Herr Kamyer and Miss Wilson. I do it only to help them with their luuurve.

    I amaze myself with my caringnosity.

Twenty-five minutes later

Ach, so here is the full-frontal *knutschen* scale.

1. *Händchen halten*
2. *Arm umlegen*

3. *Abscheidskuss* (hahahahahah, once again the lederhosen types come up trumps on the mirth-ometer)

4. *Kuss, der über drei minuten*

5. *Kuss mit geöffneten Lippen* (I don't know how Geoff got in here, but that is boys for you)

6. *Zungenkuss*

7. *Oberkörperknutschen – im Freien* (outside)

8. *Oberkörperknutschen – drinnen* (inside)

9. *Rummachen unterhalb der Taille* (*ja, oh ja!!!*)

10. *AUF GANZE GEHEN!!!*

Wednesday September 14th
Up at the crack of 7:00 a.m.

This is my plan. I set off to Stalag 14 with my uniform "customised". (My skirt turned over at the waist to shorten it, no tie and no beret.) I do my make-up and hair for max glamorosity. Do the walky walky hip hip flicky hair thing all the way to school until just by the loos in the park. By this time I am only about one hundred yards from the school gate. Then I nip into the park loos while my very besty pally Jas stands guardey dog outside. In the loos I take my make-up off, undo customised uniform, put on stupid beret etc.

Resume looking like a complete prat, then quickly walk in the middle of the Ace Gang and pass through the Gates of Hell into Stalag 14.

8:15 a.m.

Jas was sitting on her wall, chewing her fringe. If she isn't careful, she will develop furballs like cats do. Gordy was doing that choking and coughing thing last night and then he sicked up a fur ball. Disgusting really. Especially as it wasn't even the colour of his fur. I am hoping against hope it has nothing to do with licking the Prat brothers, but facts have to be faced, and he does spend an awful lot of time in their kennel with them.

They are entering a dog show soon and if I see Gordy coming to heel to Mr Next Door and wearing a little pink collar, my worst suspicions will be fulfilled. So far, Angus has not been fit enough to ride the Prat brothers around like little horsies like he did before. But when he does start again, imagine what he will do if he drops down on to Gordy's back.

When she saw me, Jas said, "Erm, you are a dead person. Hawkeye will keep you in detention for ever and you will have to write a zillion times, 'Although I look like a prozzie I am merely a tart.'" And she started honking with laughter.

She calmed down a bit when I got her in a headlock. From upside down she said, "Nurk, I am just saying that—"

I let her go because I couldn't make out what she was babbling on about and her face had gone very red. She straightened her skirt.

"I am just saying, Georgia, that when Hawkeye sees you all dolled up like a tart she will not take it kindly."

"She won't see me all dolled up. I am only all dolled up in case Masimo is anywhere in the vicinity. Before we get to the school gates I am going to make myself look like the rest of you – boring and sad."

Jas said, "Well, Tom says he likes me looking natural."

I just looked at her. "Jas, you don't look natural."

She was going to get on to the having-the-hump scale, so I quickly said, "You look bloody gorgey, that's what you look, you bloody gorgey – thing. Anyway, this is my plan. I look all glam till we get to the loos near school, then if I see Masimo all is tickety-boo luuurve-wise. However, if I don't see him, I scoot into the loos and take my make-up off and turn my skirt down etc. Ditto at home time. I nip into the loos, reapply glamorosity, turning up skirt etc., etc. You and Ace Gang huddly duddly me out of the school gates just in case there are any Hitler Youth on girl-baiting duty. Then if Masimo is there waiting for me, I am a vision of whatsit. Do you see?"

She is, of course, being all grumpy about it but she will do it.

Ten minutes later

She was saying, "I read *Rom and Jule* last night – it's so beautiful, isn't it?"

I said, "No, it's weird. It's even weirder than *MacUseless*, and that was staggeringly weird."

Jas was off in Jasland though. "It was so romantic, and you know, when everyone, the nurse and all the Capulets were saying bad things about Rom, well, Jules just stuck with him. And I think there is a lesson there for us all."

I said, "Oh yes, what is it? Don't get married at thirteen to some twit in tights?"

Jas was looking all misty-eyed. "No, it means stick to what you feel, no matter what anyone else says. And that is why I have decided not to play the elastic-band game with Tom. I just love him and he can do whatever he wants. I will just love him."

Good grief. Should I start singing and banging a tambourine? Jas has turned into Baby Jesus in a beret.

Which reminds me, I have decided to audition for Mercutio. I have many literary reasons for this: mainly, he ponces around in tights for only two scenes and then is stabbed to death. Which, as a result, leaves many, many happy hours of lolling around backstage having a hoot and a laugh with my mates. And the lads.

Rom and Jule read-through and audition in the main hall 2:00 p.m.

Miss Wilson is already hysterical.

I said to Rosie, "Certain people are not cut out to be teachers of the young."

Rosie said, "Do you mean people with out-of-control bobs?"

And I said, "Yes."

She has brought it on herself. You would have thought that after the fiasco of the orange-juggling in *MacUseless* she would have learned not to be innovative. But you just can't tell some people.

This time she has suggested we might try puppetry and mime in our production. That immediately caused an outbreak of us all pretending to be Thunderbirds puppets. Oh, we laughed.

Then, when we had almost stopped and got ourselves under control, she said that in Ye Olde Days the audience was not very quiet and would shout rude jokes and stuff out at the actors.

Rosie said, "Like Romeo, Romeo, wherefore art thy PANTS, Romeo?"

And that once more introduced the old pants theme into everything that we did. Miss Wilson only has herself to blame.

Ten minutes later

Jas was being annoyingly Jasish. She has learned all Juliet's lines for the first two acts. How incomprehensibly botty-kissing is that? She has done it because she genuinely thinks that she is Juliet.

And that Tom is Romeo.

As I said to her, "We'd better say ta taa then, Jas, because you die at thirteen. Which was two years ago."

She just stropped off to be with the others who are taking the whole thing seriously.

Ten minutes later

I was being the prologue person and I was giving it my all at the front (oo-er). I said:

"Two households both alike in dignity,

In fair Verona, where we lay our scene,

From ancient grudge break to (and I couldn't resist the comedy opportunity) new nudity,

Where civil PANTS makes civil PANTS unclean."

Oh, we laughed. I thought that Rosie was going to have a spaz attack.

Miss Wilson was yelling, "Girls, girls stop this silliness. Saying pants all the time is not funny."

It is, though.

Twenty-five minutes later

Anyway, the horrific outcome is that Miss Bum-oley Kisser Jas is in fact Juliet. This is going to be unbearable for the next few weeks. She is soooo full of herself. Discussing stuff with Miss Wilson. I actually overheard her say, "Yes, perhaps a puppet dog would add to the whole Elizabethan feel of the production. It is very likely that Juliet would have had a little dog as a companion."

Perhaps a swift rotten tomato in the gob might add to the whole Elizabethan feel.

Rosie has been cast as the nurse, which I think is an act of theatrical suicide. Ellen is Tybalt and I am Mercutio – hooray!!!

Miss Wilson had to spoil things by saying, "I am casting you, Georgia, because although you have been silly this afternoon, I know you are not going to let me or the team down."

Jas went, "Humph."

She is at number three on the having-the-hump scale (head-tossing and fringe-fiddling) and we haven't even done the first read-through yet.

Although I don't know why we are bothering rehearsing the final scenes, because with Ellen dithering around with a sword as Tybalt, it is quite likely that none of us will survive longer than Act Two.

In the loos
4:00 p.m.

I've sent Jools on a little scouting mission to see if there are any signs of an Italian Luuurve God anywhere outside the school gates. My hands are trembling a LOT and I've nearly blinded myself twice with my mascara brush. Fortunately, we haven't had to prance around like ninnies doing sport today, so my hair has retained its bounceability factor.

Ten minutes later

Jools came into the loos.

"Oh my giddygod, Gee, he's here. He's on his scooter at the gates. And he's sort of brown, and well, I mean, I like Rollo but I mean, phwoooaaar is all I can say!!! Times ten."

My bottom nearly fell out of my panties. I sat on the edge of the sink. Blimey. My heart was racing.

Thank God the prefects were having a late meeting about discipline, because I know Wet Lindsay is just waiting to get me for something. She has a plan for me and I will not be liking it. But at least she is out of the way for now.

All of the Ace Gang came into the loos. I said to them, "Right, I am ready. I want you all to metaphorically hold my hand across the playground so that I do not fall over."

Jools said, "I haven't done metaphorical hand-holding. How does that go?"

I said, "You all walk across the playground and we chat and laugh like it is normal to be meeting a Luuurve God, but while you are chatting and so on, you are also mentally holding my pandie so that I do not fall over."

Jas, who has not come down to earth since she became Jule, was still going on like Mrs Owl the Dim. "When you

240

say mentally holding your hand, do you mean we hold your hand and go mental?"

"Jas, Jas, please do not make me mess up my hair by beating you to a pulp. You know very well what I mean. Just do it."

We laughed and chatted all the way, step by step. I have absolutely no idea what anyone said, least of all me. I had never felt so nervous in my life. I took a quick look up from my casual laughing and saw him sitting on the seat of his scooter, with his long legs crossed. My heart skipped a beat; he was quite literally gorgey porgey. How could he like me? It was like being in a film.

When he saw me he got up and took off his gloves. He was wearing a pale blue leather coat and his hair had grown. And he looked so – so – Pizza-a-gogoish!

Then he did a wave and shouted, "Ay, Georgia, *ciao, cara, ciao!*" and started walking towards me and the gang.

He said to them, "*Ciao, signorinas*, and here is the, how you say, the very lovely, *molto bellissima* Miss Georgia."

And he came right up close to me and lifted me off my feet and kissed me properly and quite hard on the mouth. No warmsy upsies. Just a proper snog. And he didn't even make it a short one. I was still off my feet and I hadn't closed my eyes because I was so surprised, so I had gone slightly cross-eyed. His mouth felt lovely but not very familiar to me. Then he put me down and he kissed me quickly and said, "Oh, I have waited long for this. Come on, miss." And he took my hand and led me off to the scooter.

I turned back to the Ace Gang and they all went, "Oooohhhhhhhhhhhh get you!" in a high-pitched camp tone.

One hour later

We drove off through the streets on his scooter. It felt soooo full of glamorosity. He accelerated up the High Street quite fast. We stopped at the lights and he put down the bike stand and got off his seat, leaving the engine running. We were surrounded by cars and there were people passing by. I wondered what he was doing. Should I get off? Were we parking at the lights and going for a cup of coffee? Or did he think I should have a go at driving? Even though I can't even ride a bicycle properly.

Then he took off his helmet and he said, "I must snog you more." Blimey. And he did. He bent down and pushed up my goggles and then kissed me on the mouth. How erm... interesting. It was nice but I couldn't really concentrate because everyone was looking at us. I could see some kid in the back of a car picking his nose. People were honking their horns and some lads were going, "Get in there, my son!!!"

Masimo didn't seem to notice. He even put the tip of his tongue in my mouth, which made me go a bit jelloid. Then he said loudly, "Ah, that is better. Now I can continue. Thank you," and he bowed to the people in cars and to passers-by.

He leaped back into his seat, shoved his helmet on (without fastening the strap... I could imagine what Jas would have said about that), kicked away the bike support and revved off.

We went to the woods and it was a lovely soft warm just beginning to be autumn evening. As we went into the trees we found a little babbling brook. It was quite literally making a babbling noise as it went over pebbles and rocks. If I had to talk to Masimo any time soon that is what I would be doing – babbling.

I felt incredibly nervous. And I couldn't think of anything to say.

That was because we snogged. It was groovy gravy and I felt all melty like I didn't know the difference between his mouth and mine.

Fifteen minutes later

I am still feeling incredibly nervous and I can't think of anything to say. But that is all right because we are in snog heaven. Having a snogtastic time.

Rosie was right – foreign boys do that varying pressure. Soft and then hard and then soft again.

I wonder what would happen if we both did the same thing at once? For instance, if we both did hard together and I didn't do yielding, well, would we end up with really stiff necks? Or if I yielded when he yielded, would we both fall over? Or if he went to the right and I went to the right as well and we clashed teeth, would we – oh shut up, brain.

Funny, when I snogged normally, my brain went on a mini-break to Loonland. It didn't usually enter the debating society competition on snogging techniques.

Then Masimo stopped mid-snog and just looked me straight in the eyes. He didn't say anything, just looked me in the eyes. I didn't like to blink because it seemed a bit rude, but in the end I had to look down because my eyes were beginning to water. When I looked up he was still looking me in the eyes. He is, it has to be said, gorgey porgey times twelve.

He has really long eyelashes and a proper nose. I couldn't

even see up his nostrils. And a lovely mouth, with just the suggestion of hairiness around the chinny chin area, like a sort of designer stubble. Not like a little vole lurking around like Dad has on the end of his face. And it wasn't bum fluff like Oscar has. And it wasn't prickly like when Grandad gave me "chin pie" but it was deffo hairy stuff.

And also, I think, although I didn't like to stare like a staring thing on stare tablets, there was also a bit of chest-type hair coming out of the top of his shirt.

Blimey.

It must be brilliant to be a boy and not have to worry about suppressing the orang-utan gene. To be able to just let it grow wild and free. Of course, you can take anything too far, and some of the lads who play footie in the park are quite literally chimpanzee from the shorts downwards. I don't know about the top bit, and I don't want to know about the top bit.

Thirty seconds later
Dave the Laugh is a bit hairy as well. Anyway, shut up about Dave the Laugh; he is not in this scenario.

Ten seconds later

And Dave the Laugh is not right about Masimo being a lezzie and that is *le* fact.

Then Masimo said, "*Cara*, it is how you say nippy nungas."

I looked down at my nungas. Please God I hadn't had a sudden outbreak of sticky-out nip nips. No sign of them – phew, I was OK. I looked up again and he said, "Brrrr." And put his coat round my shoulders.

I said, "Oh, you mean nippy noodles!" And I laughed, but not in a good way, in a sort of heggy heggy hog hog way. Oh good, I am starting to laugh like my mad little sister.

One minute later

As we walked back towards his scooter, the Luuurve God said, "My – erm – other girlfriend, in Italy, I would like for you to meet her."

What what?! Am I in a *ménage à trois* (or *uno menagio d trois* –io)?

Two minutes later

It turns out that Masimo is talking about his ex girlfriend, the one I saw at the Stiff Dylans gig and the one he went out with before me. Gina. Anyway, she has met an English boy and they are going to get married! And he would like me to meet her when she comes over in a couple of weeks.

Blimey.

I hadn't done ex-girlfriend work before.

And she was getting married.

Wow.

And not like Rosie. Not a Viking marriage in twenty-five years time. But a real one. One without horns and probably not wearing a hat made out of herring.

My *How to Make Any Twit Fall in Love with You* book had better have a section on conversational hints with ex-girlfriends. You know, how to avoid past snogging chat.

I must never say, "So, what number on the snogging scale did you get up to, Gina? With my present boyfriend?" Get out of my head, past snogging scale!!!

We walked along a bit in silence holding hands. I couldn't think of anything normal to say. Then the Luuurve God said, "I am going to the Stiff Dylans' rehearsal tonight. Do you want for to come?"

Inwardly I was thinking, *Er, nothing would make me go and sit through two hours of nodding along and then going home in*

247

the equipment van and sitting on Dom's drum and falling through it. Like I did the last time I went to a Stiff Dylans' rehearsal. Dom still stands in front of his drum kit any time I go near.

There are, it has to be said, about a million reasons why nothing will make me go to a Stiff Dylans' rehearsal. In fact, I would rather be covered in frogspawn. And slightly roasted.

But I didn't say that. I said, "Erm, no, I've got homework to do."

Masimo smiled and chucked me under the chin and said, "Aaaaah, the little girl has her homework to do."

He said it in a nice way. But I still felt a bit stupid. So no change there.

I was saved from being more of *la grande idiote* because we got on his scooter and raced through town.

It is vair vair groovy being with him; all the girls look as we go by. I did a casualosity-at-all-times just lightly holding on to one of his shoulders thing. Until we went round a corner a bit fast and I had to grab hold of his helmet.

When we got to my place Masimo got off and started giving me a big snog goodbye. I could see Mum hiding behind the curtains in the front room. How vair vair embarrassing. I went a bit red and said to Masimo, "Oh God, my mum is watching us."

He looked up and smiled towards the window and then he blew a kiss and said, "Perhaps she wants to join in."

Ohmygiddygod, how horrific is that as an idea? Now I am involved in Europorn!!!

When I went into the house I heard Mum scampering into the kitchen and as I closed the door she called out, "Georgia, is that you?"

I said, "Mum, I saw your head bobbing around like a budgie."

She came out of the kitchen and said, "He is quite categorically gorgey."

I didn't say anything. I just went up to my bedroom in a dignitosity-at-all-times way.

Midnight

Ah well, Angus is on the road to recovery – he is sleeping comfortably on my head. And as a precaution against him tumbling off and waking himself up, he has his claws lightly stuck into my scalp.

Thursday September 15th

It is vair vair hard work being the girlfriend of a Luuurve God. Constant grooming is required; the public expects it. However, as I do not wish to be flogged to within an inch of my life by the fascists (Hawkeye etc.), I have not applied any make-up. Just put on a touch of foundation, lip gloss and mascara. And a teeny white eyeliner line round the inside of my eyes to make them look gorgey and marvy and uuumph.

Stalag 14

When I got to the school gates this morning Masimo was there waiting for me with a present! Honestly! How romantico is that? *Molto molto* romantico. It was a bottle of perfume from Italy called Sorrento.

I've never been bought perfume before. Libby made me some perfume from rose petals and milk but that is not the same. Especially as Gordy drank it.

All the girls were going mental, flicking their hair and doing mad pouting around him. It felt quite groovy. I was doing my shy smiling and looking up and looking down business, with just a touch of flicky hair, nothing like the other fools around me. I thought maybe he would kiss my hand and zoom off but then he snogged me! Full-frontal snogging in front of everyone. And by everyone I mean Hawkeye.

As Masimo took off she appeared like the Bride of Dracula shouting, "Georgia Nicolson!! You are an absolute disgrace and a shame to your uniform. What kind of an example are you to the younger girls, behaving like a prostitute in front of them. What on earth will they think?"

Actually, I could have told her what they thought because as I slunk off to see Slim for part two of the ranting and raving, the Little Titches passed by and went, "Coooorrrr, miss," and winked.

As Wet Lindsay escorted me to Slim's office she said, "You appalling tart. Personally I think Masimo should get some charity award for even touching you."

Oh, I hate her. I hate her so much you could bottle it.

Slim rambled and jelloided on for three million and a half centuries. "Blah blah, terrible example... blah blah... shouldn't be canoodling with boys... plenty of time for that... in my day... no canoodling until we were eighty-five etc., etc..."

RE
9:45 a.m.

When I finally escaped with double detention I went and sat down next to Rosie and she sent me a jelly baby and a note: Did the nasty jelly lady scare you with her chins?

I wrote back: No, but she did say "canoodle".

I feel a bit sick.

Art room

OK, on the dark side I have double detention, but on the bright side I am a bit perked up because I am wearing my new Italian perfume given to me by my groovy gravy boyfriend. And I am among my besties, the Ace Gang, doing an art project on the camping fiasco. Instead of proper lessons. What larks!!!

Miss Wilson is beside herself with excitement again. This has been a big week for her creativitosity-wise. First her puppet version of *Rom and Jule* and now the camping-fiasco project. Her bob is practically dancing the tango.

Jas is also vair vair excited. And she is walking funny. Sort of floating along and shaking her hair about. Why?

Thirty seconds later

Oh, I know what she is doing, she is walking in what she fondly imagines is an Elizabethan way. But actually looks like someone with the terminal droop.

She has brought in her collection of newt drawings and some jamjars of frogspawn.

I said to her, "Jas, that is not frogspawn, it is clearly a bit of snot in a jamjar." She didn't even bother to reply.

I am making a hat out of leaves.

Rosie said, "What is that?"

I said, "It is a hat made of leaves and so on. It is a triumphant celebration of the great outdoors."

Rosie said, "No, it is not. It is some old leaves and it is WUBBISH."

Yes, well, that is as maybe, but it is better than her "natural orchestra" which is essentially a bit of rice in some tins and a couple of spoons.

Herr Kamyer popped by and Miss Wilson went into a spectacular ditherama at the sight of her "*traum*boy."

I must tell her about the snogging scale in German so that she is ready, should Herr Kamyer leap on her for a spot of number three – *abscheidskuss.*

253

Five minutes later

Jas was actually humming "The hills are alive with the sound of pants" as she arranged her jamjars.

I said to her, "Jas, do you know what 'snot' is in German? It is '*schnodder*'. Comedy gold, isn't it, the German language?"

She said, "Shhh."

I said, "Do you know what shhhh is in lederhosen talk?"

But she started humming even louder.

Two minutes later

In a spontaneous outburst of madnosity Rosie has joined in with Jas's humming and started singing, "The hills are alive with the sound of pants", accompanying herself on rice tin and spoons. She was singing, "The hills are alive with the sound of pants, with pants I have worn for a thousand years!!!"

It was very infectious. I started improvising a woodland wonderland dance which involved a lot of high kicking and leaf work.

We were yelling, "I go to the PANTS when my heart is lonely—" when Herr Kamyer put his foot down with a firm hand.

He shouted, "Girls, girls, ve will not continue ze project if this kafuffle goes on!! Vat is the big funniness *mit* pants?"

We stopped eventually but I said under my breath, "*Kackmist.*" Which means buggeration. Oh, what a hoot and a half.

4:20 p.m.
Oh goddygodgod, how boring is detention. Miss Stamp was my guard. I am sure she was grooming her moustache as I wrote out, "A predilection for superficiality leads remorselessly towards an altercation with authority."

A million times (ish).

But I have my German book on my knee. Tee hee.

Canoodling is *rummachen*. Absolute top comedy magic.

5:30 p.m.
Freedom, freedom!!!

I skipped out of the school gates, and carried on doing a bit of ad-hoc skipping down the hill past the park.

Which is when Dave the Laugh emerged from the park loos!! *Caramba!* I stopped skipping but it was too late. He said, "Excellent independent nunga-nunga work, Georgia."

He had just been playing footie and was a bit sweaty. His hair was all damp. I quite liked it. He's got a nice smell.

He walked along with me and said, "What have you been up to?"

I didn't mention exactly why I had been kept behind. Well, actually, I lied. I said that I had been given detention because I had done an improvised dance to "The hills are alive with the sound of pants".

He said, "Top work."

I felt a bit bad about lying, but on the other hand I didn't want to say that I had been punished for snogging Masimo at the school gates.

Four minutes later

Dave does make me laugh. I told him about the German snogging scale and he was nodding and going, "*Oh ja, oh ja!!! Ich liebe der* full-frontal *knutschen. Ich bin der vati!*"

Then he said, "You don't fancy a spot of *rummachen unterhalb der taille*, do you? Just for old times' sake?"

I said, "Dave, how dare you speak to me like that."

And he said, "You know you love it, you cheeky *fräulein*."

I just walked quickly off. I have my pridenosity.

He caught me up and said, "Stop trying to get off with me."

I was amazed. "Er, Dave, I think you will find that it was you who asked to *rummachen*."

"No, it wasn't."

"Er, yes, it was, Dave."

"No, you thrust yourself at me. Because you cannot resist me. It is sad."

I stopped and looked at him. "Dave, I can resist you. I have an Italian Luuurve God as a boyfriend."

Dave said, "Oh, he is so clearly gay."

"Dave, he is not gay."

"He has a light blue leather coat."

"That does not make him gay; it makes him Italian."

Dave said, "I rest my case."

I looked at him. And then he just bent down and looked at me. He has lovely lips and I sort of forgot where I was for a minute. I felt my lips puckering up and... then he pushed me away from him so that I nearly fell over.

He said, "Look, Georgia, stop it, try and control yourself, you are making a fool of yourself."

I was speechless. What, what??? I didn't know what to do I was so amazed, so I shoved him quite hard. He looked at me. And then he shoved me quite hard back, and I fell over. I got up and went and shoved him again.

He said, "Look, leave me alone. Your girlfriend will be really cross and get his matching leather handbag out."

He is sooo annoying. I was just marching over to shove him again when Masimo whizzed up on his scooter.

Dave waved at him and as he went off he said, "Oooh, she doesn't look very pleased."

And in fact he was right. Masimo did look a bit cross. He smiled when I came over though and said, "*Ciao*... you are fighting with Dave?"

I said, "Erm... no, it was just that, er, he was showing me how he, er, scored a goal. And he was saying that he and his girlfriend, Emma, are coming to the Stiff Dylans gig."

Masimo looked a bit confused but then he said, "Come, I will take you for a coffee."

Coffee bar

I feel like a prat and a fool. I have just dashed to the loos to put make-up on. Funny I didn't remember I hadn't got any on when I was with Dave. So I've done the lippy mascara thing, but there is not much I can do about my uniform. I hope I don't see anyone I know.

one hour later
I tried to explain the German snogging-scale thing to Masimo and he laughed, but I don't think he really gets it.

At home in bed
Oh God, it was like twenty questions when I got home. Where have you been? Blah blah blah, school finishes at four p.m., it's now eight p.m. That's four hours gap.

I made the mistake of saying to Dad, "Dad, I am not a child.'

Then he rambled on saying stuff like, "No, you can say that again, you are not a child, you are a spawn of the Devil." etc., etc.

In my bedroom
10:30 p.m.
I tell you this: I'm not the only spawn of the Devil in my family. Some complete fool (my dad) has bought my sister (also known as the littlest spawn of the devil) a "hilarious" fishing souvenir.

 259

It is a stuffed fish on a stand and when you press a button it starts squiggling around doing a trout dance and singing, "Maybe it's beCOD I'm a Londoner" over and over again.

10:50 p.m.

Libby lobes it. It is her new besty. And new besties always sleep in my bed.

10:52 p.m.

Bibbs is fast asleep but I'm not because I have fins sticking up my nostrils.

11:00 p.m.

Also, why has she still got her wellies on?

11:05 p.m.

Oh god, now Angus has come into my room and is trying to get on to the bed.

11:12 p.m.

I'm going to have to get out of bed and haul him in. He's already crashed into the dressing table twice and is now in the wastepaper basket. I'll be glad when his tail is back to normal.

11:20 p.m.

So, here we all are then, tucked up together: Libby, Mr Fish, Angus, a jar of potted fish (Libby's snacks for Mr Fish) and me, hanging on to half an inch of bed.

11:28 p.m.

But I'm happy. I have a Luuurve God as a boyfriend!!! Yes, yes and thrice yes! Or *sì, sì* and thrice-io *sì*, as I must learn to say.

11:30 p.m.

Wait till I tell the Luuurve God about the Mr Fish episode tomorrow when he picks me up at Stalag 14. I bet he will laugh like the proverbial drain-io.

11:35 p.m.

Perhaps I will save the Mr Fish story because he didn't exactly fall about when I told him about the German snogging scale.

11:40 p.m.

Dave the Laugh did though. He thought it was a hoot and a half.

11:45 p.m.

How dare he insinuate I am a cheeky *fräulein*? If anyone's a cheeky *fräulein*, he is. And he said that I was thrusting myself after him, but it was him who asked to *rummachen*. Anyway, shut up, brain. I'm not thinking about Dave the so-called Laugh.

Midnight

I think Masimo is a bit jealous of Dave. Tee hee. I'm a boy-entrancing vixen.

12:30 a.m.

Oh, dear God, I've accidentally set Mr Fish off. How disgusting to have it writhing around in bed and singing. I will never sleep at this rate. It's like Piccadilly Cir...

zzzzzzzzzzzz.

Friday September 16th

I woke up laughing about Dave the Laugh asking if he could *rummachen unterhalb* my *taille*. Tee hee.

Not that I want him to.

The puckering up thing was just a knee-jerk reaction . Like if you think of lemons, your mouth waters. So if someone looks like they are going to kiss you, you pucker up.

It is just biological.

Nothing to worry about.

4:10 p.m.

I cannot believe this!

Wet Lindsay came up to me as I was coming out of the loos. The Ace Gang had gone on ahead because I am meeting Masimo at the school gates. She said, "Go and get your hockey kit; you have volunteered for extra practice. Miss Stamp's thrilled with you."

I said, "I think you will find that actually I haven't volunteered and that I am going off to meet my boyfriend. Do you know him? He is a Luuurve God."

She stood in front of me. "If you know what's good for you, you will get changed and get out there on that pitch."

Merde. I would just do a runner but she would only report me and then I would have to go to the elephant house (Slim's office) and be beaten to death by chins again.

I slumped off behind her.

She hasn't even got a bottom.

We passed Miss Stamp in the corridor and she said, "I am really very impressed with you, Georgia, and it is very kind of you, Lindsay, to encourage the younger girls. I will be mentioning it to the headmistress. It is a nice change to see you out of the detention room, Georgia. Keep it up."

Buggeration.

She went off into her office.

Lindsay looked at me and gave me a very scary "smile". How can Robbie snog her? It must be like snogging a cross between an octopus and a praying mantis. Erlack.

Ten minutes later

Lindsay is making me run round the hockey pitch.

She said, "Let this just be a little lesson to you, Nicolson, about how bad life can be if you cross me. Run round the pitch four times and then you can go. I'll be watching you."

I said, "Masimo will be waiting for me."

She said, "Well, you had better run like the wind, hadn't you?" And she went off into the changing rooms. I could see her looking at me through the window.

Twenty minutes later

Dear *gott in Himmel* I am shattered. I haven't got my special sports nunga-nunga holder and it is very tiring having them bouncing about. I finished the four laps and then I limped across to the changing rooms. I was so hot. I'd have a very quick shower, apply lippy etc. and then dash out to my boyfriend.

Thirty seconds later

The door was locked!

Five minutes later

I can't believe this. It's Mr Attwood's night off and no one else has a key.

I bet it's not his night off. I bet he is doing this on purpose. He is probably lurking around somewhere laughing.

Also, where is Wet Lindsay?

In the end I had to give up on getting my clothes. I will have to go home in my trackies with a massive red head. I wonder what Masimo is thinking. I wonder if he is still there? In a way I hope he isn't because I know what he will be thinking if he sees my head. He'll be thinking: *If I wanted a tomato for a girlfriend, I would have asked for one.*

As I came out of the school building I saw Wet Lindsay getting on the back of Masimo's scooter and taking off!!

What a spectacular cow and a half she is. She'd done this on purpose. She said she would get me and she has.

There is only one reasonable solution to this.

I will have to kill her and eat the evidence.

Walking home redly

My knickers are sticking to my botty. This is quite literally a PANTS situation.

Two minutes later

As soon as I get in I am going to plunge my head into a bucket of cold water.

One minute later

Although with my luck I will get my head stuck in the bucket at which point Masimo will turn up on his scooter and dump me.

Home

When I walked into the kitchen Dave the Laugh was there, balancing something on Libby's nose. What? What fresh hell?

He looked up as I came in and said, "Blimey, you're red."

I tried to walk across the kitchen doing that hip hip flicky flick thing to distract attention from my head, but unfortunately my botty hurt so much from running I couldn't keep it up.

I turned my back to him and got a drink of water. I said, "What are you doing here?"

He said, "I just brought round the kitty treats for Angus, but Libby has eaten most of them. Still, it's the thought that counts."

I turned back to him and he looked at me. "You are quite sensationally red."

I went off into the bathroom.

He was not wrong. I looked like my head had turned into a lurking lurker.

Five minutes later

I quickly plunged my head into icy water and towel dried my hair into what I hoped was a tousled yet somehow strangely attractive style (that is what I hoped). Quick bit of lippy and mascara. I didn't want to be in the tarts' wardrobe too long in case Dave the Laugh decided to go. I expected he had

267

come round to apologise for his awful behaviour *vis à vis* the *rummachen* incident.

Back in the kitchen
Two minutes later

I said to Dave, who was now having his hair plaited by Libby, "I suppose you have come to apologise for the *rummachen* fiasco."

And he said, "*Nein.*" Which made me laugh. He started to say, "Look, Georgia, I wanted to say that—"

At which point Mum came mumming in, talking rubbish.

She was adjusting her basoomas and flicking her hair. Surely she didn't think that Dave fancies the "more mature" lady??

She said, "Dave do you want to stay for tea? It's cool if you want to hang out for a bit."

It's cool if you want to hang out for a bit? What is she talking like a complete fool for? Oh, hang on, I think I know the answer to that one.

Dave said, "No, I'm afraid I'm away laughing on a fast camel. People to see, old people to rob, that sort of thing." And he got up to go.

Libby clung to his neck as he got up, like a toddler limpet –

just hanging round his neck. He started walking off as if he hadn't noticed he had a toddler necklace and Libby was laughing and laughing. She said, "I lobe my Daveeeeeeeeeeeeeeeeee."

Blimey, she's joined the Dave the Laugh fan club as well.

I walked Dave to the gate, trying to get Libby to let go.

As I was pulling her off Masimo turned up on his scooter. He took his helmet off and sat on the seat, looking at us. Maybe he was mesmerised by my head. It still felt vair hot. I tried to do a bit of flicky hair but it was mostly sticking to my scalp.

Dave said, "*Ciao*, Masimo."

And Masimo said, "*Ciao,* mate."

But I am not entirely sure he meant the "mate" bit.

Dave scarpered off quite quickly and Libby started burrowing through Mr Next Door's hedge. She likes to go and sit in the kennel with the Prat Poodles and Gordy. But I can't worry about that sort of thing now.

Masimo looked a bit upset and he said, "Why did you not for me wait?"

I babbled on, "Well, Wet Lindsay said I had to do extra hockey, so I had to run like a loon on loon tablets round and round, like a hamster with trackie bums on, and then I was locked out, and I saw you driving off with her on the back."

Masimo said, "Aaaah. She said you had gone home and could I give her a lift."

Unbelievable!!! What a prize tart she is!!

Masimo was smiling a bit now. He really was gorgey porgey. He said, "And Dave, he came here, for you to have another fight?"

I laughed. "No, he came to bring some kitty treats for Angus but Libby ate them."

Masimo held out his arms. "Come here, miss."

I went over to him and he said, "You are very, erm, slippery."

Actually, he was right. If he squeezed me too hard I might shoot out of his hands like a wet bar of soap.

Then he kissed me. Which was fab and marvy and also number four, with a touch of virtual number five.

And that is when Dad came roaring up in his loonmobile.

I stopped kissing Masimo and leaped away from him like he had the Black Death. I said to the Luurve God; "Quickly, save yourself, my father is here. You must go now while you can, otherwise he may show you his leather trousers."

But it was too late. Vati had got out of his "car" and was bearding towards us. Oh how embarrassing. He was going to say something. I knew he was. Even though I have told him he must never address me in front of people.

He said, "Evening all. It's Masimo, isn't it? Are you coming in?"

Oh nooooooo.

I said, "No, Masimo has to go. He is rehearsing."

Masimo looked at me and I opened my eyes really wide and said, "Aren't you?"

He got it and said, "Ah, yes, *ciao*, Mr Nicolson. *Grazie*, but I must now to go. The Stiff Dylans are playing this weekend."

Dad said, "Oh well, maybe I will pop by to hear some tunes, come along and show you a few of my moves on the dance floor."

Has he snapped?

Masimo revved up his scooter. He leaned over and kissed me and said, "I will see you Saturday. I am, how you say, missing you already."

I tried to walk off in a dignity-at-all-times sort of way, but as we got to the house Dad yelled to Mum, "Georgia has been snogging an Italian stallion."

How disgusting!

I feel dirty and besmirched.

And also *kackmist*.

In bed

I wonder what Dave the Laugh was going to say to me? He does make me laugh. It was vair amusing, him sitting there having his hair plaited by Libby.

Anyway, I will ask him what he was going to say when I see him at the gig.

One minute later

If I get the chance. I expect he will be with his girlfriend.

Which is good.

And fine.

Two minutes later

I know that Emma is nice and everything but she did have a ludicrous spaz attack when Angus accidentally spat at her. Which is a bit weedy.

Anyway, I have vair many other important things to worry about. If Dave the Laugh wants to go out with a weed, that is his right. But the burning question is this: what in the name of Richard the Lionheart's codpiece am I going to wear for the gig?

Five minutes later

All the girls will be looking at me because a) I am officially going out with a Luuurve God and b) I am a multi-talented backing dancer and jolly good egg.

Fisticuffs at dawn

Saturday September 17th

8:30 a.m.

Preparations begin to become the girlfriend of a Luuurve God.

And possibly backing dancer.

So first on my list is cleanse and tone.

Done.

Face mask.

Done.

Cucumber eye patches.

Done.

Plucking.

Yessiree Bob.

Puckering exercises.

Done.

Lunch

Two jam sandwiches for max energy and nutrition.

Ellen was eating fruit gums in maths on Friday and Hawkeye asked her why, and Ellen said, "It is my breakfast." Hawkeye nearly had a complete ditherspaz and f.t. combined.

She said, "Where is the nutrition in that?"

And Ellen said, "Well, because of the, you know, erm... fruit or something."

3:00 p.m.

Charming conversation practice.

Done.

(Note to loon brain headquarters: do not mention hilarious pants jokes, full-frontal *knutschen*, glove animal or horns.)

6:00 p.m.

I think I look quite fab and groovy. That is what I think. Hair bouncing around, nungas more or less under control. And

 275

I've got new special lash enhancing mascara on so my lashes are about two foot long. Of course I will never ever be able to get it off again but in the meantime I have max boy entranceability.

6:30 p.m.
If I can't get the mascara off by Monday it will give Wet Lindsay an excuse to attack me with a blow torch or put me on gardening duty with Elvis for the rest of my life.

She's bound to be there tonight. Poncing around like a ninny.

If I get a chance to warn Robbie about her I will. I must be cunning and full of subtlenosity.

Clearly, I would rather just rip her stupid octopussy head off to save time. But there is bound to be some busybody goodie-goodie who would complain to the RSPCA about it.

Leaving Home
7:15p.m.
Dad and Uncle Eddie were tinkering with the Robinmobile as I went off. They are both wearing T-shirts with a picture of Uncle Eddie in his baldy-o-gram costume on the front of them. And underneath the picture it says, "He dares to

baldly go where no other man has baldly gone before."

Good grief.

At the Honey Club
8:30 p.m.
Quick check in the tarts' wardrobe.

Looking in the mirror. Hmmmm. Hellooooooo, Sex Kitty. Grrrrrr.

A quick splosh of my perfume from Italy that my Italian boyfriend brought me from Italy, which is to the right on the map from Merrie Olde England. Possibly. And then my public is ready for me.

Out in the club by the bar
Sven and Rosie have excelled themselves. Their theme tonight is fur, fur with just a hint of fur. Did you know you could get matching fake-fur jumpsuits? In purple? Well, you do now.

I am a bit nervy actually. This is like my first official outing as the official girlfriend of a Luuurve God. Still, I have my Ace Gang to keep me company.

Ten minutes later

Blimey, I am goosegog girl because all the rest of the gang are with their "boyfriends". Even Ellen. Although she might be the last to know – or something.

Rom and Jule (otherwise known as Jas'n'Tom) are all over each other like a rash. It is quite sweet really. If you like that sort of thing.

No sign of Dave the Laugh and his girlfriend. Which is cool. They have probably gone out somewhere different. How should I know?

They might be round at Emma's.

You know. Messing about and so on.

I seem to want to go to the piddly-diddly department again.

In the tarts' wardrobe

Oh marvellous, Wet Lindsay and Astonishingly Dim Monica are in front of the mirrors. I don't know why they are bothering. Lindsay would need a head transplant to make her look less like Octopussy Girl.

One thing for sure, I am not going into a cubicle and doing a piddly diddly while they are looking at me.

Back in the club

I said to Rosie, when she was on a snog break, "I wonder where Masimo is?"

She said, "Why don't you go backstage in your capacity as girlfriend and say to him, 'I just came to say break a leg,' or whatever you say to rock stars? Maybe it's 'break a string' or 'break your trousers'. I don't know, but just go say it."

And then I saw the Stiff Dylans come in with their guitars. They must be due on soon. As soon as they appeared they were surrounded by girls. Or "tarts" as some people might call them.

Two minutes later

The Stiff Dylans are signing autographs. Honestly! Actually signing autographs. I can see the Luuurve God. He is there signing as well. And smiling and chatting to the girls. I wonder if I should go out and get my coat and then come back in again like I have just arrived? I could sneak out and—Then he looked up and saw me. He waved and started coming over. Hurrah!

Blimey. He has an amazingly cool suit on. I bet it is from Pizza-a-gogo land. When he reached me he put his arms

♡ 279

around me and kissed me. Everyone was looking. I felt a bit red actually. I haven't done much public snogging. He didn't even seem to notice the crowd around us. He was just looking in my eyes and he said, "*Ciao, cara*, I will see you at the break, and then after the gig we go maybe to somewhere we can be together?"

Blimey O'Reilly's trousers, it's a bit early to get swoony knickers but I have got them on.

one hour later

The whole place is rocking. The Stiff Dylans have played a cracking set and Robbie has just gone on stage to join them. He is doing sharesies vocals with Masimo on "Don't wake me up before you go. Just go." I wonder if Robbie wrote that for Octopussy Girl?

I would.

She is standing looking at him right at the front of the stage. I said to Jas, "How uncool is that?"

She was too busy smooching with Hunky to bother to reply.

Lindsay has given me the evils since I got here but I am not at school now, and also I am with my mates. And also I am the girlfriend of a Luuurve God.

Which is a bit weird actually. Loads of girls that I don't even know have been coming up to me and saying, "Oooh, isn't he gorgey, what is it like going out with him? What kind of music does he like? What is his birth sign?" etc.

What am I? His press secretary?

I didn't mention to them that I am in fact a backing dancer.

Half an hour later

This is more like it. The Ace Gang rides again!! We are doing a shortened version of the Viking disco hornpipe to "Ultraviolet" by the Dylans. We haven't got any props so we are having to improvise the paddles and so on. It is a hoot and a half.

I waved my (pretend) paddle at Masimo, but he didn't wave back. I suppose it's a bit difficult when you are playing a guitar. He looked at me though. I like to think in an admiring way.

Two minutes later

Another fast one by the Dylans. Everyone is going mental.

And Dave the Laugh is here!!! I only saw him when he came up to me and said, "Let's twist!!" And he started doing this mad fast twisting thing, going down to the floor and then up again. Quite sensationally insane, but funny. He was yelling at me, "Come on, Kittykat. Get down!!!"

I said, "Not in a million years. Get your girlfriend to make *le idiot* of herself."

He shouted, "She's not here. You can be substitute idiot!! Come on, you know you want to!!!"

Sven and Rosie and the whole gang joined in. So in the end so did I. It was the best fun!

Ten minutes later

I am hotter than a hot person on hot tablets. And that is hot, believe me. The Dylans are just going off for a break and Dave the Laugh has gone to get us some drinks.

Two minutes later

I was so full of exhaustiosity that I sat on Ro Ro's knee. She was sitting on Sven's knee so it was like a knee sandwich.

I said to her, "You have a vair comfy knee, little matey."

And she said, "Are you on the turn?"

I was just about to hit her when Masimo came up to me and said, "Georgia, come outside with me."

Rosie said, "Oo-er."

And just at that moment Dave came back with the drinks. He handed me a glass and went, "Yeah, groove on! Nice set, mate."

Masimo smiled, but not a lot, and then he said. "You are enjoying dancing with my girlfriend... mate?"

Dave said, "Oh blimey, this is not fisticuffs at dawn, is it?"

Masimo looked a bit puzzled. He said, "What is this fisticuffs?"

Dave put his drink down on the table and started prancing around doing his impression of Mohammed Ali crossed with a fool. He was yelling, "I am sooo pretty, I float like a butterfly. Duff duff. Put em up, put em up."

He is, it has to be said, bonkers.

I was laughing. We were all laughing. Except Masimo. He said to Dave, "Oh, I see. OK. We can do it this way. I will see you outside. Mate."

Dave said, "I'm afraid I am not a homosexualist."

But Masimo handed his jacket to me and started walking towards the door.

Surely he was joking.

Dave looked at me and shrugged. And then he went outside as well. Blimey.

Jas said to me, "I told you that your big red bottom would get you in trouble and now... you see."

What what???

I'd just been doing the twist, Masimo didn't even know about the accidental nearly number five in the woods scenario. I followed them both as they went out of the doors.

In fact most of the people in the club followed us outside.

Outside

Masimo said to Dave, "OK, now we sort this out, man to man."

Were they actually going to fight over me?

I should have liked it. But...

Rosie said to me, "This is just like Rom and Jule, isn't it? If they were wearing tights. Should we lend them some?"

I said, "Look, look, lads, this is silly. Why don't you just..."

Masimo was still looking at Dave and he put up both hands like they do in movies and started circling Dave, saying, "Come on."

Jas said, "Georgia, say something! Do something normal and sensible for once."

Yes, yes, that is what I must do – display maturiosity.

I stepped into the middle of them both and yelled, "STOP!!! STOP... IN THE NAME... OF PANTS!!!"

Masimo just looked at me. But Dave the Laugh started falling about laughing. And Rosie started singing, "The hills are alive with the sound of PANTS! With PANTS I have worn for a thousand years!" And then the Ace Gang joined in.

Two minutes later

Everyone was drifting off now that there was no chance of a fisticuffs extravaganza.

Dave was still laughing. He turned to Masimo and held out his hand and said, "It's just a little joke, mate, nothing to get your handbag out for." Then he said, "Night night, Gee," and went off.

I smiled at Masimo, but he didn't smile back. He looked at me and he looked really sad.

Donner *und* Blitzen.

And also *pipi*.

And *krappe*.

I started to go over to him and he turned away from me and walked off into the night.

Two minutes later

My Luuurve God has got the hump.

In fact he has just quite literally had the full Humpty Dumpty.

But maybe it will just be an overnight hump and in the morning all will be well again.

I wouldn't mind, but I've only been the girlfriend of a Luuurve God for about a month.

And I haven't seen him for most of that time.

Has he really dumped me?

One minute later

Just because I did the twist with Dave the Laugh.

And had a German fight with him.

And accidentally snogged him in the Forest of Red-bottomosity.

Which the Luuurve God doesn't know about anyway.

Two minutes later

Oh marvellous, I am once more on the rack of love with no cakes.

All aloney on my owney.

Again.

PANTS.

Georgia's Backing Dancer Portfolio

In case you haven't noticed, me and the Ace Gang (and when I say me and the Ace Gang, I really mean me) have created some of the grooviest dance moves ever invented. I have always found that a quick burst of disco inferno dancing is a fab way to get rid of tensionosity and frustrated snoggosity. So, because I love you all so much – and also because, like me, you may be considering a career as a backing dancer – I have made a portfolio of my favourite moves. Starting with dances from the early days.

The Simple Years
"Let's go down the disco"

This was really an ad-hoc dance fandango. The main thrust and nub was that when a so-called teacher turned their back to illustrate something on the board, we all leaped up and did a brief burst of disco dancing, then sat down before we got multiple detention.

The Middle Years

1. The Viking bison disco inferno

We're still practising this for Rosie's forthcoming (i.e. in eighteen years time) Viking wedding. It is danced to the tune of *Jingle Bells* because even Rosie, world authority on Sven land doesn't know any Viking songs. Apart from *Rudolph the Red-nosed Reindeer*. Which isn't one.

For this dance you need some bison horns. If you can't find any bison shops nearby, make your own horns from an old hairband and a couple of twigs or something. Oh, I don't know, stop hassling me, I'm tired. It goes...

Stamp, stamp to the left,
Left leg kick, kick,
Arm up,
Stab, stab to the left (that's the pillaging bit),
Stamp, stamp to the right,
Right leg kick, kick,
Arm up,
Stab, stab to the right,
Quick twirl round with both hands raised to Thor (whatever),

Raise your (pretend) drinking horn to the left,

Drinking horn to the right,

Horn to the sky,

All over body shake,

Huddly duddly,

And fall to knees with a triumphant shout of

"HORRRRNNNNN!!!!"

p.s. In a rare moment of comic genius, Jas, who is clearly in touch with her inner bison, added this bit too. It's a sort of sniffing-the-air type move. Like a Viking bison might do. If it was trying to find its prey. And if there was such a thing as a Viking bison.

Stab, stab to the left,

And then sniff sniff.

Hahahahahaha!

2. The snot disco inferno

For this dance you will need a big blob of bubble gum hanging off your nose like a huge bogey. It needs to dangle about so you can swing it round and round in time to the music. Dance this to your favourite TV show theme tune. It goes...

Swing your snot to the left,
Swing to the right,
Full turn,
Shoulder shrug,
Nod to the front,
Dangle dangle,
Hands on shoulders,
Kick, kick to the right,
Dangle dangle,
Kick, kick to the left,
Dangle dangle,
Full snot around,
And shimmy to the ground.

Yes, yes and thrice yes!

The Maturiosity Years
The Viking disco hornpipe
And finally, the piece of resistance and cream of the cream –

the Viking disco hornpipe extravaganza!!! For this you need bison horns, mittens, ear muffs and paddles. Do remember muffs are worn *over* horns, not horns over muffs. You will feel like a fool and a twerp if you muff it up. Danced to the tune of *EastEnders*, it goes...

The music starts with a Viking salute. Both paddles are pointed at the horns.

Then a cry of "Thor!!!" and a jump turn to the right.

Paddle, paddle, paddle, paddle to the right,

Paddle, paddle, paddle, paddle to the left.

Cry of "Thor!!!" Jump turn to the left.

Paddle, paddle, paddle, paddle to the left,

Paddle, paddle, paddle, paddle to the right.

Jump to face the front (grim Viking expression).

Quick paddle right, quick paddle left x 4.

Turn to partner.

Cross paddles with partner x 2.

Face front and high hornpipe skipping x 8 (gay Viking smiling).

Then (and this is the complicated bit) interweaving paddling!

Paddle in and out of each other up and down the line, meanwhile gazing out to the left and to the right

(concerned expression - this is the looking-for-land bit).
Paddle back to original position.
On-the-spot paddling till all are in line and then close eyes
(for night-time rowing effect).
Right and left paddling x2 and then open eyes wide.
Shout "Land Ahoyyyyy!"
Fall to knees and throw paddles in the air (behind, not in
front, in case of crowd injury).

Excellent in every way!

For more marvy extra stuff from moi, visit

www.georgianicolson.com

- ♪ join the Ace Gang
- ♡ download gorgey stuff
- ♪ win fabbity-fab prizes
- ♡ sign up for monthly G-mails from Georgia
- ♪ post photos of your bestest pallies on the gallery
- ♡ chat to chums on message boards
- ♪ and much, much more!

The Having-the-Hump Scale

1. ignorez-vousing

2. sniffing *(in an I-told-you-so way)*

3. head-tossing and fringe-fiddling

4. cold-shoulderosity work

5. Midget Gems all round, but not for you

6. pretendy deafnosity

7. walking on ahead

8. the quarter humpty *(evils)*

9. the half humpty *(evils and withdrawal of all snacks)*

10. the full Humpty Dumpty *(walking away, leaving behind that slight feeling that you have been dumped)*

The New and Improved Snogging Scale

1/2. sticky eyes (*Be careful using this. I've still got some complete twit following me around like a seeing-eye dog.*)

1. holding hands

2. arm around

3. goodnight kiss

4. kiss lasting over three minutes without a break (*What you need for this is a sad mate who's got a watch but no boyfriend.*)

4 1/2. hand snogging (*I really don't want to go into this. Ask Jas.*)

5. open mouth kissing

6. tongues

6 1/2. ear snogging

6 3/4. neck nuzzling

7. upper body fondling - outdoors

8. upper body fondling - indoors

Virtual number 8. (*When your upper body is not actually being fondled in reality, but you know that it is in your snoggees head.*)

9. below waist activity (*or bwa. Apparently this can include flashing your pants. Don't blame me. Ask Jools.*)

10. the full monty (*Jas and I were in the room when Dad was watching the news and the newscaster said, "Tonight the Prime Minister has reached Number 10." And Jas and I had a laughing spaz to end all laughing spazzes.*)

Georgia's Glossary

arvie · Afternoon. From the Latin "arvo". Possibly. As in the famous Latin invitation: "Lettus meetus this arvo."

billio · From the Australian outback. A billycan was something Aborigines boiled their goodies up in, or whatever it is they eat. Anyway, billio means boiling things up. Therefore, "my cheeks ached like billio" means – er – very achy. I don't know why we say it. It's a mystery, like many things. But that's the beauty of life.

Black Death · Ah well... this is historiosity at its best. In Merrie England, everyone was having a fab time, dancing about with bells on (also known as Maurice dancing), then some ships arrived in London, full of new stuff – tobacco, sugar, chocolate, etc., yum yum. However, as in all tales in history, it ended badly, because also lurking about on the ships were rats from Europe – not human ones. And they had fleas on them that carried the plague. The fleas bit the people of Merrie England, and they got covered in pustulating boils and died. A LOT. As I have said many many times, history is crap.

Blimey O'Reilly · (as in "Blimey O'Reilly's trousers") This is an Irish expression of disbelief and shock. Maybe Blimey O'Reilly was a famous Irish bloke who had extravagantly big trousers. We may never know the truth. The fact is, whoever he is, what you need to know is that a) it's Irish and b) it is Irish. I rest my case.

blodge · Biology. Like geoggers – geography, or Froggie – French.

Boboland · As I have explained many, many times English is a lovely and exciting language full of sophisticosity. To go to sleep is "to go to bobos", so if you go to bed you are going to Boboland. It is an Elizabethan expression... Oh, OK then, Libby made it up and she can be unreasonably violent if you don't join in with her.

brillopads · A brillopad is a sort of wire pad that you clean pans and stuff with (If you do housework, which I sincerely suggest you don't. I got ironer's elbow from being made to iron my vati's huge undercrackers.) Where was I? Oh yes. When you say "It was brillopads" you don't mean "It was a sort of wire pad that you clean with", you mean "It was fab and groovy." Do you see? Goodnight.

bum-oley · Quite literally "bottom hole". I'm sorry but you did ask. Say it proudly (with a cheery smile and a Spanish accent).

chuddie · Chewing gum. This is an "i" word thing. We have a lot of them in English due to our very busy lives, explaining stuff to other people not so fortunate as ourselves.

clown car · Officially called a Reliant Robin three-wheeler, but clearly a car built for clowns by some absolute loser called Robin. The Reliant bit comes from being able to rely on Robin being a prat. I wouldn't be surprised if Robin also invented nostril-hair cutters.

clud · This is short for cloud. Lots of really long boring poems and so on can be made much snappier by abbreviating words. So Wordworth's poem called "Daffodils" (or "Daffs") has the immortal line "I wandered lonely as a clud". Ditto *Rom and Jule*. Or *Ham*. Or *Merc of Ven*.

double cool with knobs · "Double" and "with knobs" are instead of saying very or very, very, very, very. You'd feel silly saying, "He was very, very, very, very, very cool." Also everyone would have fallen asleep before you had finished your sentence. So "double cool with knobs" is altogether snappier.

Eccles cake · A culinary delight from the north of England. Essentially they look like little packets of dead flies, yum yum. Lots of yummy things come from the north of England: cow heel and tripe (a cow's stomach lining with vinegar). And most delicious of all, cow's nip nip (yes I am serious). What you have to remember is that the northern folk are descended from Vikings and, frankly, when you have been rowing a boat for about three months, you will eat anything.

fandango · A fandango is a complicated Spanish dance. So a fandango is a complicated thing. Yes, I know there is no dancing involved. Or Spanish.

full-frontal snogging · Kissing with all the trimmings – lip to lip, open mouth, tongues... everything (apart from dribble, which is never acceptable).

f.t. · I refer you to the famous "losing it" scale:
>   1. minor tizz

2. complete tizz and to-do
3. strop
4. a visit to Stop Central
5. f.t. (funny turn)
6. spaz attack
7. complete ditherspaz
8. nervy b. (nervous breakdown)
9. complete nervy b.
10. ballisiticisimus

gadzooks · An expression of surprise. Like for instance, "Cor, love a duck!" Which doesn't mean you love ducks or want to marry one. For the swotty knickers among you, "gad" probably meant "God" in olde English and "zooks" of course means... Oh, look, just leave me alone, OK? I'm so vair tired.

goosegog · Gooseberry. I know you are looking all quizzical now. OK. If there are two people and they want to snog and you keep hanging about saying, "Do you fancy some chewing gum?" or "Have you seen my interesting new socks?" you are a gooseberry. Or for short, a goosegog, i.e. someone who nobody wants around.

gorgey · Gorgeous. Like fabby (fabulous) and marvy (marvellous).

Hoooorn · When you "have the Horn" it's the same as "having the big red bottom".

in vino hairy arse · This is a Latin joke and therefore vair vair funny. The Latin term is "*in vino veritas*" which means "truth in wine". That is, when you are drunk you tell the truth. So do you see what I've done??? Do you? Instead of "veritas" I say "hairy arse". Sometimes I exhaust myself with my amusingnosity.

Jammy Dodger · Biscuit with jam in it. Very nutritious(ish).

jimjams · Pyjamas. Also pygmies or jammies.

Midget Gem · Little sweets made out of hard jelly stuff in different flavours. Jas loves them A LOT. She secretes them about her person, I suspect, often in her panties, so I never like to accept one from her on hygiene and lesbian grounds.

Mystic Meg · A mad woman in a headscarf and massive earrings who can predict the future. And probably lives in a treehouse. A bit like Jas really. Except that Jas hasn't got a headscarf or earrings. And can't tell the future. Apart from that (and the fact that Mystic Meg is a hundred) they are quite literally like identical twins.

nippy noodles · Instead of saying "Good heavens, it's quite cold this morning," you say "Cor, nippy noodles!!" English is an exciting and growing language. It is. Believe me. Just leave it at that. Accept it.

nuddy-pants · Quite literally nude-coloured pants, and you know what nude-coloured pants are? They are no pants. So if you are in your nuddy-pants you are in your no pants, i.e. you are naked.

nunga-nungas · Basoomas. Girls breasty business. Ellen's brother calls them nunga-nungas because he says that if you get hold a girl's breast and pull it out and then let it go, it goes nunga-nunga-nunga. As I have said many, many times with great wisdomosity, there is something really wrong with boys.

Pantalitzer doll · A terrifying Czech-made doll that sadistic parents (my vati) buy for their children, presumably to teach them early on about the horror of life.

Pizza-a-gogo land · Masimoland. Land of wine, sun, olives and vair vair groovy Luuurve Gods. Italy. The only bad point about Pizza-a-gogo land is their football players are so vain that if it rains, they all run off the pitch so that their hair doesn't get ruined.

red-bottomosity · Having the big red bottom. This is vair vair interesting *via-à-vis* nature. When a lady baboon is "in the mood" for luuurve, she displays her big red bottom to the male baboon. (Apparently he wouldn't have a clue otherwise, but that is boys for you!!) Anyway, if you hear the call of the Horn, you are said to be displaying red-bottomosity.

Rolf Harris · An Australian "entertainer" (not). Rolf has a huge beard and glasses. He plays a didgeridoo, which says everything in my book. He sadly has had a number of hit records, which means he is never off TV and will not go back to Australia. (His "records" are called "Tie Me Kangaroo Down, Sport," etc.)